A Hamburger Christmas

A Detectives Daniels and Remalla Novella
J. T. Bishop

Eudoran Press LLC

Eudoran Press LLC
6009 W. Parker Rd. Su. 149-193
Dallas, TX 75093
www.jtbishopauthor.com

Publisher's Note: This is a work of fiction. Names, characters, places, and incidents are a product of the author's imagination. Locales and public names are sometimes used for atmospheric purposes. Any resemblance to actual people, living or dead, or to businesses, companies, events, institutions, or locales is completely coincidental.

Author Photos by Nick Bishop and Mayza Clark Photography
Book Editing by P. Creeden and G. Enstam, C. Marquis and C. McGuire.
Cover Design by J.T. Bishop
Photo credits: anyaberkut, unkreatives, and YAYimages
A Hamburger Christmas/ J.T. Bishop -- 1st ed.
ISBN: 978-1-955370-21-9

Other Books by J. T. Bishop

To my family. We've been blessed with many happy Christmases for which I am deeply thankful. This one's for you.

Chapter One

SIMON CREPT QUIETLY THROUGH the dark, empty house. His brother, Gary, followed behind him. "Egg was right," whispered Simon. "Nobody's home."

Gary shoved him from behind. "Did you think Egg was lying?" he whispered back.

Simon shook his head. "No."

"Then shut up and hurry."

Simon walked rapidly through the kitchen and into the living room. The tall, dark Christmas tree, its lights off but the ornaments still twinkling from the reflection of a dim hall light, stood beside the window. Gifts, some stacked on top of one another, surrounded it.

Gary whistled. "Jackpot."

Simon stopped, and Gary walked around him. Holding his gun, Gary eyed the gifts as if they were his. He set the gun down on a coffee table. "Let's dig in." He kneeled and grabbed a gift.

The familiar guilt bloomed, and Simon's heart fell. "Do we have to?" Anticipating his older brother's reaction, he flinched.

Gary glared at him. "What the hell is the matter with you? This is why we're here." He ripped open a package. "We find something good, and we get paid." After removing the gift wrap, he tossed it aside, opened the box and pulled out some scarves. He cursed and tossed them aside. "Worthless." He paused and stared at Simon. "C'mon. Get busy. We don't have all night." He reached for another gift. "You want to get caught and go to jail?"

Reluctantly, Simon kneeled next to his brother. "I hate this part." He reached for a gift and tugged on the bow.

"I don't know why you care. People who live like this can replace this stuff in a heartbeat." He opened another package and grunted when he saw slippers. "And it's not like we're getting any gifts at home, so we have to make our own luck." He tossed the slippers aside.

Simon thought of his mom, who worked two jobs and when she was home, was either drinking, with a man, or both. She routinely told them she had enough money for their basic needs, but the rest was up to them, and Christmas and birthday gifts were for the wealthy. Simon wondered how she had enough to spend on her liquor, but he'd learned the hard way not to ask about that. He unwrapped the large gift and read the side of the box.

Gary glanced over and his eyes widened. "Oh, hell, yeah. That's what we're looking for." He slid it over. "A VR gaming system. Egg's gonna love that." He pushed it behind him.

Simon couldn't help but think of the disappointed kid who wouldn't be getting his VR set on Christmas morning. "We could leave it behind."

Gary smacked his brother on the side of the head. "You're an idiot. Keep looking." He ripped open a small package and smiled. "Earrings." He pulled them out and they sparkled in the dim light. "We'll take these, too." He put them back in the box and set them on top of the VR.

Simon wished he'd stayed home, but then remembered why he hadn't. His mom was home tonight with her new boyfriend, Desmond, who'd asked Simon after his second date with his mother to call him Dad. His mother had laughed and Simon, using a colorful expletive, had told Desmond what to do with the tequila bottle he'd been holding.

Desmond had grabbed him by the arm, and Simon had anticipated the slap, but his mother had stopped Desmond, telling him to keep his hands off her son. If anyone was going to punish him, it would be her. Then she'd told Simon to take his ugly mouth and get lost. He'd left and found Gary hanging out with his friend, Egg, on the corner. They'd been talking and Gary was mad Simon had interrupted them, telling him he had no business being out there, but Egg had taken a look at Simon and had asked his age.

Gary had told him Simon was fifteen and Egg, with a big smile, convinced Gary to let his little brother in on the conversation, which Simon quickly discovered was about the ease of breaking into homes. Egg explained that if Simon or Gary, who was seventeen, got caught, they'd only go to juvenile detention, and after they turned eighteen, their record would be cleared, and it would be like starting over.

They'd committed their first break-in a week later.

Egg had prepared them. He'd told them what neighborhoods to target, when to break in, what to look for, what to do if an alarm went off, and if they were caught, how to handle it. He usually suggested the targets but recently, since getting out of school for the holidays or ditching it altogether, Gary had chosen a few of his own. Egg had given them a phone number, made them memorize it, and if they were arrested, they were to call the number and keep their mouths shut.

Once they had the loot, they were to bring it to him. He'd sell it and they'd get a percentage. So far, in the weeks prior to Thanksgiving when they'd been hitting homes, they'd made five hundred dollars which they'd split between them, but Egg had promised them the big money would come at Christmas time. And he was right. Right after Thanksgiving, they'd started robbing houses with big lighted trees in the window and lots of gifts beneath them.

Some were easy and others more difficult, but the more they did it, the better they got at it, and the biggest scores were when they found a quiet, dark home with no alarm. They could take their time, open the gifts, and see what they could take, and this one was one of the more lucrative targets.

No matter how many times they did it, though, Simon couldn't shake the guilt. He couldn't help but think of the kids whose Christmases he was ruining. Just because he and Gary had a lousy Christmas didn't mean they had to make other kids' holidays lousy, too.

Gary opened another gift and discarded a fluffy robe.

Simon thought of his mom. "We should keep that."

"Egg said electronics and jewelry only." He shoved the robe aside.

"We could give it to Mom for Christmas."

Gary hesitated and snickered. "What the hell for? It's not like we're getting anything from her. Besides, if she sees that, she'll know we stole it. How else could we afford it?"

Simon had to admit that was true. "Okay." He opened another gift and found a popular video game.

"Add it to the pile," said Gary.

Simon tossed it next to the earrings.

"Pull out the bag," said Gary.

Simon stood and grabbed a plastic bag from his pocket. He opened it and tossed the gifts they were taking with them inside of it. He heard Gary whistle again.

"Look at this." He eyed a shiny silver watch. "Egg's gonna love this haul." He put the watch in his pocket.

"You keeping that?"

Gary shrugged. "Maybe."

"What for?"

"Cause I want to, idiot."

"Egg finds out you're holding out or someone else sees it, and we're in trouble."

Gary stood and shoved him. "You let me worry about that, and I didn't ask you."

Simon suspected the truth. "Is that for Trey's Dad?"

Gary narrowed his eyes and sharpened his tone. "I told you to mind your own business, stupid." He grabbed the plastic bag. "Let's get out of here before they come home."

Simon noted the flicker of sadness that crossed his brother's face. "He doesn't need or want the watch." He paused. "And none of what happened was your fault."

Gary erupted. "I told you to shut up." He yanked the plastic bag up and hooked it over his arm. "I'll smack the shit out of you if you say another—"

Lights brightened the windows and created shadows in the room. Glancing out the window, Simon saw headlights as a car pulled up into the front driveway. "They're home."

"Shit. Let's go." Gary grabbed his gun and tucked it into the back of his pants. "Hurry."

Following his brother, Simon ran to the back of the house and out the back window. They stopped long enough to put on their dark ski masks and then took off toward the back gate, where they darted into the alley and disappeared into the night.

Chapter Two

Captain Frank Lozano leaned back in his chair at his desk and rubbed his weary eyes. His stomach rumbled. He eyed the banana on his desk but preferred the chocolate chip cookies from the vending machine. He rubbed his belly and wondered when he could escape his office long enough to snag the snack.

"Hungry, Cap?" asked Aaron Remalla, one of his detectives. He and his partner, Gordon Daniels, were in his office discussing the latest robbery in a string of them. They'd begun before Thanksgiving, but since then, they'd picked up in regularity, Christmas gifts being the target.

Lozano watched Remalla chow down a chocolate donut in less than a minute and wasn't sure if he was disgusted or jealous. "I'm good, Remalla."

Remalla wiped his face with a napkin. "Want me to get you a donut?"

Lozano glared at him. "No, I don't want you to get me a donut."

"Still trying to lose the extra ten?" asked Remalla. He licked his thumb.

"Would you leave the man alone?" asked Daniels, who sipped his apple juice. Daniels was a healthy eater who hit the weights at his gym, dressed decently, and took care of himself. Remalla was the opposite. He ate what he wanted, didn't much care about how he looked, and maintained his trim physique with an occasional long run. Despite their opposite approaches to life, Daniels and Remalla were as close as brothers and two of his best detectives, although they sometimes drove Lozano nuts.

Remalla picked up his Styrofoam cup loaded with cream, sugar, and some coffee. "What's the big deal? He's hungry."

"You know he's trying to watch what he eats. Stop trying to knock him off the wagon. Offer him a granola bar or something." Daniels sipped his juice.

"You only live once," said Remalla. He winked at Lozano. "You let me know if you want that donut, Cap."

"He's got a banana right there." Daniels waved at Lozano's desk.

Remalla huffed. "I'm just saying—"

"Would you two shut up about my eating habits," yelled Lozano. "What I do and do not eat is none of your business."

"See?" said Daniels to Remalla. "Lay off the donut talk." He ran his fingers through his gelled blond hair. "I'm on your side, Cap. You want more fruit?"

Fruit was the last thing Lozano wanted. "Forget the fruit, Daniels." He shot a look at Remalla. "And forget the donut."

Rem shrugged. "Suit yourself. But if you change your mind..."

Daniels rolled his eyes.

Lozano leaned forward in his seat. "Why don't you two use those so-called brains of yours to discuss something useful. Where are we on the latest break-in?"

Daniels set his juice on the floor beside his chair. "We don't have much. It's the same as the others. They're in and out and don't leave much behind."

"Except a big mess," added Remalla. "This time they got through most of the gifts and left the gift wrap in a pile beneath the tree. They must have known the family was gone."

"That's not true for all the robberies, though," said Lozano.

Daniels shook his head. "No, it isn't. Usually, they don't hang around. They open just the obvious - the big gifts or the very small ones or they go straight for the jewelry in the house. This robbery was at night but now that Christmas is getting closer, they're starting to hit during the day, too, when the family's out."

"They're casing the houses," said Remalla. "They know who's home and when."

"They don't case them well enough to check for alarms, though," said Daniels. "If the alarm goes off, they grab whatever they can in two minutes, and then they disappear."

"They're smart, whoever they are," said Remalla. He drank some coffee.

"Anything from that video?" asked Lozano.

"Nothing," said Remalla. "Just grainy footage of two guys with dark masks and dark clothes running through a yard. They disappeared into the alley."

Daniels rested his ankle on his knee. "That seems to be their preferred exit. Running through an alley."

"You'd think the masks they're wearing would arouse some suspicion." Lozano's belly rumbled again, and he eyed the banana.

"I suspect once they hit the alley, they take the masks off and walk down it like they belong there," said Remalla. He swiped at a drip of chocolate on his shirt.

"They only take what they can carry," said Daniels. "They park nearby, get to their car, and take off."

Rem pointed. "And if anyone were to ever call the cops on them, they'd be long gone before they arrived."

Lozano swiveled in his seat. "That's just it. No one's caught them in the act or reported anything suspicious. How do they stroll down an alley, carrying what they've stolen, and nobody sees them?"

"Well, nobody's paying much attention in an alley," said Daniels.

"Cap's right, though," said Remalla. "At some point, with the number of robberies ticking up, you'd think they'd encounter someone, either driving or putting out their trash."

"I guess they've just been lucky," said Daniels.

Lozano rubbed his jaw. "We all know that at some point, their luck is going to run out. Someone's going to interrupt them or see and report them."

"And that's when we'll catch 'em." Remalla tucked a long strand of black hair behind his ear.

"At the rate they're going, Christmas will be over by then." Lozano made another mental note to stop at the store on the way home and pick up his wife's gift. "We're a week out before the holiday. That's plenty of time to do a lot of damage."

"The news reported on the crimes the other night." Daniels rolled his eyes again when his partner picked at the chocolate stain on his shirt and licked his finger. He looked back at Lozano. "The tip line has been active. Maybe something will pan out."

Lozano tapped at a file on his desk. "You think these two are working alone?"

Daniels and Remalla glanced at each other. "We doubt it," said Remalla.

Daniels nodded. "Somebody's tipping them off with where to go, what to steal and how to elude the cops. It's got to be more than these two guys."

Lozano figured as much. "So once we find one, we find the others. The whole organization will come tumbling down."

"Let's hope," said Remalla. "But you know they'll be told not to talk."

"Well, that's what I have you two for," said Lozano. "To use those sparkling communication skills of yours and get some answers."

"We've got to catch them first," said Remalla.

"And hopefully soon," added Daniels. "Or several Christmas trees are going to be a lot lonelier this year."

"Plus several disappointed kids." Lozano loosened his tie. "Let's just pray they make a mistake, and we catch them before the holiday and not on it." He groaned. "Sheila won't be thrilled if I end up having to work."

"If we don't," said Daniels. "they may lay low for a while, and who knows if we'll find them after that."

"They won't lay low forever," said Rem. "Once the money runs out, they'll be back." He fiddled with his coffee lid. "We'll get 'em eventually."

Lozano grunted. It had been a busy month and he was looking forward to a few days off. "The sooner, the better."

"You and Sheila staying home this Christmas?" asked Daniels.

Lozano nodded. "Yes. The in-laws are coming to our place this year. Gonna be a full house. What about you and Marjorie?"

Daniels picked up his juice. "We're spending Christmas with her family."

"Not going home?" asked Lozano.

"God no," said Daniels. "Why torture myself?" He uncapped his juice and drank some.

"Christmas with her family?" asked Lozano. "That's a big step."

Daniels bounced his foot. "It is but it's good. At this point I know her family pretty well."

"Glad to hear it." Lozano spoke to Rem. "You going to Florida to see your mom?"

Remalla picked at a seam in the pantleg of his jeans. "Nah. I'm staying here."

Daniels frowned. "You are? I thought you said you were going to fly out for a couple of days."

"I changed my mind."

Lozano noted Remalla's shift in body language. His swagger faded, and his shoulders slumped. "You're staying in town, then?" Lozano worried for his detective. It was his first Christmas after the death of his girlfriend and almost fiancée, Jennie, who'd died nine months earlier in a car accident.

Rem sat up in a likely attempt to look unbothered. "Didn't feel like traveling." He showed his palm to Daniels. "And before you say anything, I know you'll invite me to join you and Marjorie, but there's no need."

Daniels furrowed his brow. "Well, of course we'd invite you. I don't want you to spend Christmas alone."

"It's fine. I'm not glass. I won't break. Besides, I won't be alone. My cousin Chico invited me to his house on Christmas Eve. Said I could spend the night and hang out."

Daniels didn't look convinced. "Chico? Is that the one who made it big in the stock market? Did I meet him?"

"You did. At that hot dog eating contest I took you to."

Daniels raised a finger. "Now I remember." He squinted. "How many hot dogs did he eat?"

"Twenty-six, before he barfed them all up."

"That's right." Daniels paused. "That was a special moment."

"I thought so, too. His plan is to break his record next year."

Daniels glanced at Lozano. "And this is the man who made his fortune in stocks."

"Doesn't mean he can't shove a load of dogs down his throat," said Lozano.

"He's got a big house now, too." Rem smiled. "He had a huge housewarming party last fall. Jennie and I—" He stopped, his face tightened, and he cleared his throat. "...we, uh, went to the party." He took a second and blew out a heavy breath. "Anyway, his family will be there Christmas Eve, plus he's got other cousins coming over, so I'll stay there. I'll go home Christmas day," he looked at Daniels, "so if you want to get together then, that's fine."

Daniels studied him. "You're sure?"

"I'm sure. Stop worrying."

"You're always welcome at my house, Remalla," said Lozano. "Sheila would love to have you. Just don't bring those barbecued apple fritters that you brought for Thanksgiving."

"Those are my cousin Margot's favorite," said Rem. "She gave me the recipe."

"I tried one," said Daniels. "She obviously doesn't like you much."

Lozano chuckled. "No offense, but Sheila gave them to the dog after you left."

Rem smirked. "That's probably why Margot got tossed out of culinary school."

"No doubt," said Daniels.

"Anyway," said Rem. "I appreciate the invite, Cap, but I'll be fine."

Lozano exchanged a look with Daniels. Lozano knew Daniels was as concerned as he was, but there was little they could do. Grief was a companion that rarely left, no matter how old its presence became. "If you change your mind, you know where I am."

"Me, too," said Daniels.

"Thanks." Rem swirled his drink.

Lozano sat forward. "If there's nothing else, then you two can go. Just keep me posted on any updates."

"Will do, Captain." Daniels stood along with Remalla.

Rem headed toward the door. "With any luck, we'll crack this case before the holiday, and we can all dream of sugar plum fairies come Christmas Eve."

"Better put in a request to Santa. Maybe he or his elves can help us out," said Daniels.

"I'll see what I can do." Rem opened the door, and they left the office.

Chapter Three

DANIELS RETURNED TO HIS desk while Remalla warmed up his cup of coffee from the half-filled pot at the machine.

Daniels sat and studied his partner's back. The familiar worry rose. He knew this would be a difficult holiday for Rem, especially since the previous Christmas, he and Marjorie had spent Christmas Eve with Rem and Jennie, and then Rem had spent Christmas Day with Jennie and her family. Everyone had assumed that by this Christmas, Rem and Jennie would either be engaged or even married. "How come you didn't mention your change in plans?"

Rem didn't turn around. "Because I knew what you'd do." He added sugar to his cup. "And I don't want to be a third wheel." He stirred his coffee.

"You wouldn't be a third wheel. Marjorie would be happy for you to join us. And you've met her parents. They love you, too."

Rem dropped his disposable spoon in the recycle can and turned. "Listen. You and Marjorie have something special. You should enjoy your time with her, without having to worry about me."

"I'm going to worry about you regardless, but I'd worry less if I knew you were okay."

Rem leaned back against the cabinet. "Well, let me break it to you. This holiday is going to suck no matter where I am or who I'm with. I'll be at my cousin's, and I'll do my best not to sink into a depression, although I may have a few shots of something strong on Christmas Eve, if not a whole bottle."

"That's what I'd like to avoid. You getting drunk is not going to help."

Rem sat at his desk. "Well, it sure as hell can't make it much worse." He stared off. "I just want to get past Christmas, deal with the hell of New Years, start the next year and pray it's better than the one before it."

"How can it not be?"

Rem held his head. "God. I don't know, and I don't want to know."

"It won't be worse. I'd say you've gotten past that much." The memories of the night Jennie died swirled, and Daniels' stomach knotted.

Rem spoke softly, "I suppose."

"How about this then? You and I can get dinner Christmas Eve. Just you and me. Then afterward, I can go meet up with Marjorie and you can go to your cousin's."

Rem smiled but still looked sad. "Nope. Again, I appreciate it, but you need to be with Marjorie. And to be honest…" He sighed and studied his coffee cup. "…I think that might be worse. It would remind me too much of last year."

Daniels understood. "I didn't think of it like that. You're right. No dinner then." He recalled their fun previous Christmas Eve. The four of them had made dinner at Rem's, drank a lot of wine, laughed a lot, and had opened their gifts for each other. It had been a memorable night. "That was a fun evening, wasn't it?" He instantly regretted his words. "Sorry. I shouldn't have brought it up." He hated how the weight of Jennie's death clouded everything. He could only imagine how hard it was for Rem.

Rem looked up from his coffee. "Don't do that. We talked about this. We can't walk around and act like she didn't exist. Jennie was a big part of both our lives. It's okay to discuss the past. I'll go crazy if we have to walk on eggshells every time she's mentioned."

Daniels nodded. "Okay. I hear you." He paused. "I was just thinking that last year was one of my best Christmases ever. It sure as hell was better than any I've ever spent with my family."

Rem's smile brightened. "It was great, wasn't it?"

"I especially liked the Magic Eight Ball you got me." Daniels chuckled at the memory.

Rem chuckled, too. "You were a little freaked out over how quickly you were falling for Marjorie. I thought maybe it could give you a little insight."

"I was definitely a little freaked out, especially since I'd just met her."

"As I recall, the Eight Ball had the answer. When you asked if she was the one, it said 'Without a Doubt.'"

Daniels remembered. "Leave it to the Magic Eight Ball."

Rem turned somber again. "'Course, it said the same about me and Jennie, so it's not a hundred percent."

"It wasn't wrong. She was the one. Just not the only one."

Rem spoke gruffly. "I doubt I can handle another one."

"Not now, you can't, but one day you will."

"I'm not holding my breath."

Daniels fiddled with a pencil on his desk. "What about you? Was last year your best Christmas?"

Rem pursed his lips. "Last year was great, but there's another memorable one that comes to mind." He paused. "It ties for my best and worst Christmas."

Daniels sat up. "Now I'm curious."

Rem held his coffee. "I was thirteen or maybe fourteen. By then, my relationship with my dad had deteriorated to the point where we barely spoke, not that it was difficult since he wasn't home much. He was either working or at the bar drinking. And when he was home, he and my mom were fighting."

Daniels recalled Rem's stories about his dad. He didn't tell many about his father's issues. To others, he kept it close to the vest, telling them only that his father had died peacefully after living a good life.

Rem wiped off a drop of coffee on his desk. "Christmas was coming, and my dad was going through one of his atonement phases. He was going to do better. He was going to be the husband and father we deserved. Blah, blah, blah. Said he was going all out for Christmas. He was taking us to a hotel on the beach, there'd be steak for dinner and our favorite gifts under the tree. I have to admit. I was excited. I'd hoped this was the turnaround Mom and I were longing for." He stopped and traced a finger down a pile of paper on his desk.

Daniels leaned in. "I'm sensing it didn't turn out well."

"You win the million dollars." Rem rocked in his chair. "Mom and I went to this hotel, which was nowhere near the beach but decent enough. It had a kitchenette and two bedrooms. Dad was going to bring everything and meet us there, but he never showed."

"Oh, boy." Daniels slumped.

"So, Mom and I are sitting in this hotel with no food, no gifts, and no tree on Christmas Eve. She tried to locate him, but we knew he was in a bar, getting drunk." He studied his coffee. "By eight o'clock, I was furious and hurt and just sat in the corner, disappointed. She told me to get up though, and we went across the street where there was a big grocery store that was still open. I sulked and waited in the car while she shopped. After she came back, we returned to the hotel, and she pulled out the groceries. She made hamburgers, bought a small battery-operated tree and some cherry pie. We went out to the pool, ate the burgers while the tree blinked, and we stared up at the stars. I gave her my gift, which was a pendant she'd wanted, and she gave me the pocketknife I'd been wanting." He looked up. "We called it our hamburger Christmas."

Daniels had experienced plenty of lousy Christmases with his family but none quite like that. "That was a favorite?"

Rem nodded. "We ate our hamburgers and pie and talked. I tried to hide my anger and pain at Dad, but she knew. It was a nice night though and there was something oddly special about it. Before we went to bed, she asked to borrow my pocketknife. I thought it was strange, but I gave it to her. The next morning, we got up and were getting ready to leave the hotel when she gave me another gift. It wasn't even wrapped; it was in a grocery bag. Anyway, I opened it, and it was a plaque."

"A plaque? Like you hang on the wall?"

"Yeah. It wasn't much. Just a small square piece of flat wood with a simple border around it. She'd found it in the arts and craft section in the store. She'd used my knife to carve a message into it."

Daniels tipped his head. "What did it say?"

Rem rested his elbows on his desk. "It said, 'Trust me. Things will get better. I promise. Love, your mom.'" He set his jaw. "She knew what I needed to hear. At that point, I didn't know how I was going to put up with my dad for the next four years." He released a long breath. "And she was right. It did get better."

"Moms usually know." Daniels sat back. "What happened to the plaque?"

"I put it on the wall in my room. It stayed there until the last big fight I had with my dad. I was eighteen. I'd had enough. I broke all my dad's liquor bottles and he grabbed that plaque and stomped on it." Rem paused. "That was my sign. I left home and didn't look back."

"I don't blame you."

Rem shrugged and seemed to shake off the memories. "So, yeah. That Christmas was the worst and the best." He chuckled sadly. "Mom and I still ask each other every year if this is a hamburger or steak Christmas." He glanced up at Daniels. "Last year was steak and this year is definitely hamburger."

Daniels slid a paper aside on his desk. "It's not all bad. Your initial hamburger holiday was one of your best."

"I suppose." He set his coffee down and rubbed his face. "What about you? If last year was your best, what was your worst?"

Daniels thought back on his younger years. "Nothing as dramatic as yours. When I was little, Christmases were fine as I recall. But then I got older. Once I hit thirteen, Dad thought I was too old to expect gifts. Thought it was unnecessary and childish. I couldn't even mention Santa without him scoffing at me. Mom argued with him about it, but he didn't relent and of course, she gave in. That year, I was into gardening. I would help Mom in the backyard with the planting and did the weeding. I liked it and wanted to start an herb garden. I spotted a starter kit in a nursery and asked for it for Christmas." Recalling that crappy year, he was surprised when his old grudges resurfaced. "I remember I went to the hardware store one day with my dad, which he owned."

"He had a chain of them, right?"

"Yeah. Still does." Thinking back, he stared off. "We were at the register, and I spotted one of those silly Chia Pets on the counter. You know, the thing that's shaped like an animal and grows grass like hair?"

"Yeah," said Rem. "I had one of those things. Killed it within two weeks."

Daniels picked up a pen and gripped it. "I made some comment about how it would be neat to have, and Dad told me I needed to grow up. The time for silly gifts was over. Mom had told him about the herb garden, and he couldn't understand why I would want it. I needed to realize that Christmas was just a commercial holiday, and I wasn't a kid anymore. Wanting a Chia Pet only told him that I was immature and that as his son, he expected a lot more from me." He cursed under his breath. "Mom still gave me the herb garden kit but after that conversation with my Dad, I never used it."

Rem smirked. "Your Dad was as big an asshole as mine. He just substituted work for alcohol."

Daniels agreed. "After that year, Christmas was never the same. I was always trying to measure up, to act grown up enough for him, but I could never do it." He huffed. "Do you know we never took pictures at Christmas? I can't think of a single photo I have with my family during the holidays."

"Maybe that's for the best. There are some things that shouldn't be remembered."

"I guess that's true."

"Gotta love the holidays," said Rem. "It seems they either make you or break you."

"I suppose that's true, too."

Rem set his coffee cup down and picked up a folder. "Maybe we should get back to this case. Try and do something productive. Make your Dad proud."

Daniels snorted. "That ship sailed a long time ago." He rifled through some papers. "But you're right. We need to keep plugging and hope our burglars make a mistake."

Rem scratched his head. "That's another worry. So far, we've been lucky. It's just been break-ins, but something tells me if they're confronted, this could take a bad turn."

"You mean armed robbery? You think they're carrying weapons?"

Rem raised a brow. "They're burglars. Wouldn't you?"

"That's the last thing we need."

"Somebody surprises them at the wrong time then forget about armed robbery. We could be talking murder." He opened the folder. "And then, Santa or no Santa, it won't just be Lozano working on Christmas."

Hoping that wouldn't be the case, Daniels accessed his computer and got back to work.

Chapter Four

THE MORNING OF CHRISTMAS Eve, Simon slept until noon. After waking and rolling out of bed, he sauntered into the kitchen. It was quiet and no one was around. Eyeing the refrigerator, he spotted a note from his mom and read it.

I'm working today and spending the night with Desmond. Will be back later tomorrow to celebrate Christmas. Love you both, Mom.

Simon crumpled the note and tossed it in the trash. He grabbed a pop tart and walked into the cramped living room. A small sparse tree stood in the corner with one string of lights on it and nothing beneath it. Sad, Simon sat on the couch and wondered where Gary was. He wasn't in bed when Simon woke. Thinking he'd call, he went into the bedroom to grab his outdated cell phone when it rang. Seeing it was Gary, he answered. "Hey."

"You up, lazy bones?"

"Yeah."

"Good. Then get your ass to Egg's. We're talking. He's got a job for us."

Simon frowned. "A job? But it's Christmas Eve."

"So?"

"Everybody will be home."

"Not everybody. Come on. We can get one last score in before we start talking about our plans for after the holidays. Eggs got some ideas."

Simon almost sighed into the phone but stopped himself. He knew Egg was a bad influence on his brother, and Simon had gone along for the ride mainly to keep an eye on Gary, but at some point, they'd need to move on. Gary would be eighteen in seven months. If he got caught after that, it would be jail time, not juvie time.

"What is it? You got a problem?" asked Gary.

Simon may have only been fifteen, but he was smart enough to realize that Gary's involvement with Egg had more to do with what had happened with Trey, their cousin and Gary's best friend. Gary was angry at the world and at himself, and was expressing his pain through robbing others. The world had taken from him and now he was taking from the world. If Simon couldn't get Gary to stop hanging out with Egg, he feared Gary would graduate to something much worse than burglary.

"No. No problem. I'll get dressed and head over."

"And don't lag. We don't have all day."

"Fine," said Simon, but he spoke to dead air because Gary had hung up. He set the phone down, quickly finished his pop tart and got dressed. Five minutes later, he was on his bike and headed to Egg's. Egg lived in a small apartment not much bigger than the one Gary and Simon lived in with their mom, but there were more people hanging around. Simon figured Egg had his fingers in a lot more pies than just burglaries.

Pedaling, Simon recalled their week. After their big score where the owner had returned and they'd almost been caught, they'd hit three more homes. After each one, Simon and Gary would meet Egg at a storage facility. Egg would take the items, make a deduction in his head, and then give him and Gary their take. Simon had no idea what happened to the stolen stuff after they left it nor how much Egg actually sold it for, but he figured Egg was getting a much bigger percentage than he or Gary were. The items in the storage unit never seemed to stay for long and Simon assumed Egg got rid of it fast.

Simon had also seen a few other friends assisting Egg at the storage site. They looked as intense as Egg and didn't talk to anyone except Egg. Whatever Egg did outside of selling stolen goods, Simon didn't want to know, but he worried Gary did. And if Gary continued to hang with the wrong crowd, there was no telling what path he could find himself on. That worried Simon the most.

After arriving at Egg's, he knocked on the door. It opened and Gary pulled him inside. "What took you so long, chump?" asked Gary. "It's Christmas Eve. Egg's got things to do."

Simon eyed the messy apartment. There were pizza boxes and liquor bottles scattered on the floor, the walls were bare, and the furniture minimal. A woman was in the kitchen cleaning dishes. She wore long gold earrings, a halter top, a short skirt, and had a lot of hair spray in her teased hair.

Egg came out of the bathroom, drying his hands with a towel. "There's my man," he said to Simon. "Merry Christmas." He was tall and skinny and wore silver chains around his neck. He tossed the towel on a lumpy sofa and smiled, revealing a gold front tooth.

"Merry Christmas," said Simon. He stuck close to Gary since he never felt safe around Egg.

"Egg's got a job for us tonight," said Gary. "Says it's perfect."

"Sure do," said Egg. "I think you're going to like it."

Simon wondered what the perfect target on Christmas Eve could be. After their busy week, he figured they were done for now. "What is it?"

Egg pulled out a piece of paper from a pocket. "A house at this address. It's big, beautiful, and empty. Plus, no alarm." He handed the paper to Gary.

Gary frowned. "What about gifts?"

Egg patted Gary's shoulder. "You think I'd steer you wrong? The owners are opening their goodies today before they take off on a trip." He grinned. "Which means they'll leave plenty behind for you to scavenge, and the place is yours to enjoy for the night." His eyes sparkled. "I bet you there will even be leftovers in the fridge."

Gary dropped his jaw. "You mean we can stay there?"

Egg chuckled. "Why the hell not? Just don't advertise it. Close the curtains, don't leave fingerprints behind, and park behind the house in the alley. This time of year, everybody's visiting, so a different car won't rouse suspicion." He put an arm around Gary. "Your Mom might give you a lousy Christmas, but not your buddy Egg. I take care of you."

"Are you sure it's okay to spend the night?" asked Simon. He had to admit staying at a nice house for Christmas and maybe getting some decent food and even dessert sounded nice.

Egg smirked. "Just don't be stupid and get home before your Mom wonders where you are. Don't leave her waiting until she calls around, looking for you." He eyed the woman in the kitchen. "Darcy and I have our own plans. Don't we, baby?"

The woman in the kitchen looked toward them. "You bet we do, Sugar."

"All right," said Egg with a chuckle. He glanced back at Gary and Simon. "Any questions?"

"What time can we get there?" asked Gary.

"Make it late. I'd say around midnight. Then enjoy your Christmas. Go through the house. Maybe load up the trunk with a few high-ticket items in case you have to make a quick getaway and take something for yourself. Enjoy your Christmas. The owners won't be back for a couple of days, so no rush."

"Cool," said Gary.

"You call me Christmas morning and we'll arrange a time to meet at the storage unit. Then you can spend the rest of Christmas with your momma. It will be a Merry holiday for all of us." He put an arm around each of them. "You two have been my holiday helpers, and I pay my helpers well." He squeezed them and Simon fought the urge to push back. "I don't forget my elves," said Egg. Simon's stomach turned and he wanted to leave.

"That sounds great, Egg." Gary held up the paper. "We won't let you down."

Egg let go of them and fiddled with a sparkly bracelet on his wrist. "I know you won't G-man." He stared at Simon and Simon felt a chill run through him. Egg's eyes narrowed and his stare conveyed his ruthlessness. "I know you won't."

ell

Daniels finished the report, closed the screen, and flipped off his monitor. The squad room was quiet and he noted the empty desks. It was the morning of Christmas Eve and most of the other detectives had gone home. Lozano's office was empty, and Rem hadn't come in that morning. Knowing his partner and how he routinely waited to buy his gifts at the last minute, Daniels had told him to take Christmas Eve off. Daniels had offered to come in, finish the paperwork, and tie up any loose ends before leaving himself. There'd been plenty to deal with since there'd been three more robberies that week, and no breaks in the case. At this point, Daniels was thinking their burglars were done for the season and who knew when they'd return. It had been frustrating. Plus, as the days had ticked closer to the holiday, Rem had become quieter and his mood more somber. Daniels realized he was just counting down to Christmas and the closer it got, the harder it became.

He'd tried again to invite Rem to join him and Marjorie at Marjorie's parents, but without success. Rem had agreed though to have dinner with them Christmas night, and Daniels had taken him up on that. They could have a quiet meal at Daniels' place and exchange gifts. Daniels figured that was the best he was going to get. He was glad at least that Rem would be at his cousin's and wouldn't be alone.

He straightened the items on his desk, threw his pen in a drawer, grabbed his jacket, and stood. He'd told Marjorie he'd be done by lunch and would pick her up on his way out, and then they'd head to her mom's, who was only about thirty minutes away. Thankfully, Daniels got along way better with Marjorie's family than he did his own.

Sliding his jacket on, he left the squad room and headed down the stairs to the main entrance. Shorty, the tall, thin officer who frequently worked up front, was talking to a man at the counter. Daniels waved. "Merry Christmas, Shorty. I'm on my way out."

Shorty smiled and waved. "You have a good one, Daniels. Merry Christmas to you, too."

Daniels smiled and headed toward the exit.

"Detective Daniels?"

Hearing his name, Daniels turned. The man at the counter had swiveled toward him. He was familiar but Daniels couldn't place him.

"He's looking for Rem," said Shorty. "I told him he didn't come in today."

Holding a wrapped gift, the man approached Daniels. "You remember me?" he asked. He was burly and had wide shoulders and short legs. He wore a fancy brown leather jacket and when he smiled, his perfect white teeth stood out against his olive skin. An image of hot dogs and a vomit-filled trashcan flashed in his mind.

"Chico?" he asked, stepping toward the man. "Rem's cousin?"

Chico nodded. "I'm obviously memorable."

Daniels shook his hand. "That contest was hard to forget."

"As was the aftermath." He laughed. "I'll do better next year." He let go of Daniels' hand and patted his belly. "I'm getting lots of practice."

Daniels laughed, too. "It must be the Remalla gene. Nothing gets between you and food."

"I keep trying to convince Aaron to join the contest. I know he loves hot dogs as much as I do."

"The key difference being he likes them in his stomach. Not out of it." He pointed. "You offer him a Taco del Fuego contest, though, and he might go for it."

Chico's eyes widened. "I love those things. Best taco in town."

Daniels had never understood the appeal. "What brings you to the station? Everything okay?"

Chico waved a hand. "Everything's great. Better than great actually. The market is treating me well."

"So I've heard. How's the new house?"

"Not so new anymore. We've been in it almost fifteen months, but it's fantastic. Never thought I'd own a home like that. Life's been good to me." He opened his leather jacket. "Mona got it for me for Christmas."

Daniels felt the smooth leather. "It's very nice."

"Thanks." He closed the jacket and held up the wrapped package. "We opened our gifts after breakfast and now me, Mona and the rest of the family are headed out. I stopped by to give Aaron his gift. I figured it would be nicer to give it to him face to face, instead of just leaving it at the house."

Daniels hesitated. "You're not going to see him? Aren't you all getting together at your house tonight?"

"We thought about it but decided to head out of town early instead. Take advantage of our days off. I invited Aaron to join us, but he said no. Said he wanted to keep it quiet this year, which I get." His voice softened. "It's going to be a tough one for him."

Daniels quickly deduced that Rem had left out some of the details about visiting his cousin. "He's staying at your place?"

"He is. Said it would be good to get a change of scenery for a day or two. Plus, with the string of burglaries you guys are dealing with, it can't hurt to have a detective nearby."

"I hear you." Daniels sighed. "I tried to get him to hang out with me, too, but he said no. But he told me he wasn't going to be alone."

"That sounds like him. He doesn't want anyone to worry. I wasn't sure about it either, but I figure everyone grieves differently, and if he needs some time to himself, I'll honor it. I'm just surprised he wanted to stay at my place." He paused. "The last time he was there was for the housewarming party. He brought Jenny."

"I heard. It must have been a fun party."

"It was great. Had lots of friends and family over." His jovial look softened. "I remember at some point, we were running low on booze, so I asked Aaron to grab some more liquor from the shed out back." He leaned in. "It's a big shed, so I sort of turned it into a mancave."

Daniels nodded.

"He went out to get it but disappeared for a while. I went to go find him and caught him and Jenny making out." He chuckled. "I'd had plenty to drink, so I told everyone and the two of them got teased for the rest of the party." His chuckle tapered off. "It was a good night."

"Sounds like it."

"We're doing some updating after the holidays, so that shed will be torn down soon. I figured, maybe he wants to reminisce a little."

Daniels figured the same, and Rem could do it without anyone watching. "I still hate that he wants to be alone. No one should be alone at Christmas."

Chico smoothed out some tape on the gift. "I remember when my stepmom died, and that first Christmas after, we took my dad out of town, just to help with the memories. We went to the beach and on Christmas Day, all he did was sit on the porch by himself and stare out at the water. I don't think getting away helped."

"At least he wasn't alone."

"He was, though, in his own way." He tugged on the collar of his jacket. "Personally, I think we got on his nerves. He didn't like people hovering."

"Sounds like Rem."

"It does." Chico raised the gift. "I figured he'd be working this morning, but I guess I missed him."

"I told him to take the day. You know how he is with his gift buying. Plus, he needed it."

"We're on our way out of town. I suspect you'll see him before me. Would you mind giving this to him? Tell him I stopped by?"

"That's no problem at all." Daniels took the gift. "I'm supposed to have dinner with him tomorrow night."

"Thanks. I appreciate it." He waved. "You have a nice Christmas."

"You, too. Have a good trip."

"Thank you. I plan to." Chico started to leave.

Daniels paused and then turned. "Chico, hold up."

Chico stopped and looked back.

While Daniels understood Rem's decision to be alone, he figured his partner didn't have to be alone the whole time. "Would you mind giving me your address?"

Chapter Five

REM ENTERED CHICO'S QUIET house through the front door. It was Christmas Eve, the sun was down, and Santa was supposedly in full swing with his gift giving. Holding his knapsack, plus a couple of grocery bags, he moved through the large home and entered the living area. A big tree stood in the corner, and the skirt around it was bare. Chico and his family had already opened their gifts. A dim light was on in the kitchen, and Rem walked toward the counter which faced the open living room. He set the bags down and put his knapsack on the floor.

He opened one of the grocery bags and took out the food and six-pack of beer he'd bought at the store. He added it to the fridge amongst the leftovers and then grabbed the other bag. He'd kept himself busy on purpose. Intentionally leaving all his errands to the last minute, he'd gone shopping, buying all his gifts that day. Then he'd gone home, wrapped them, threw some overnight stuff in his knapsack, and had stopped at the grocery on his way to the house.

Staying occupied had helped, but now that he was here, and his errands finished, he felt the same heavy feeling return. As hard as he tried to ignore it, it was impossible. He told himself he just had to get through today and tomorrow, and then he'd deal with New Year's. And assuming he'd survive it, he'd move on, taking it a day at a time.

He opened the second bag and pulled out the gifts for Chico and his family and set them down. Seeing the ones for Daniels, he decided to leave them in the bag. He would give them to Daniels tomorrow. Eyeing the tree, he picked up Chico's gifts, walked over and set them beneath it. Chico could open them when he got back. Rem plugged in the cord to the tree lights, and they came on and twinkled in the dark room.

Telling himself that it was just another night and to take it easy, he grabbed his knapsack and the other bag and found the room down the hall where he would be sleeping. He dropped both items in the bedroom closet and shut the door, then wondered what to do next. Should he just go to bed and get Christmas Eve over with? Noting the time, he saw it was only eight o'clock. It was too early, and he didn't expect to sleep anyway. Instead, he returned to the kitchen and grabbed a beer out of the fridge. Spotting a small tree on a side table, Rem walked over and seeing a button on the stand, he pressed it. The tree came to life with music and lights. He hit the button again and the music turned off, but the lights remained on. He hit the button once more and they turned off. He admired the other festive decorations in the room before he sat on the sofa and watched the lights on the big tree flicker. He didn't bother turning on the overhead lights. Something about sitting in the dark seemed fitting.

Drinking his beer and listening to the quiet, he couldn't help but think back to the last time he'd been there. It had been Chico's housewarming. He'd brought Jennie and after they'd both had a few drinks, Chico had asked him to grab some more liquor from the shed in the backyard. Rem had obliged, and Jennie had followed him out. After entering what Chico called a shed, though, he had to stop and admire it. It was the nicest shed he'd ever seen. There was a couch and a TV, plus extra chairs and a small bar and cabinet where the alcohol was kept. Rem had sat on the couch, and Jenny had joined him. They'd talked about how nice it would be to have a house of their own one day. At the time, they were living in his small apartment without much space for the two of them.

Rem had promised her that one day, they'd be having their own housewarming party and he'd have his own man cave like Chico. She'd laughed and asked about her space, and he'd told her she could share his whenever she wanted. She'd argued that if it was their shared space, it couldn't be a man cave. It would have to be their couple cave, special only to them. He'd grinned and asked what they would do in their couple cave and she'd smiled slyly, kissed him, then whispered in his ear exactly how they could use it. His body reacting, he'd forgotten about the party and kept up the kissing, and if Chico hadn't interrupted them, they'd have done much more on that couch.

Smiling at the memory, a twinge plucked at his heart and the familiar ache returned. Missing Jenny, he ran a hand through his hair and groaned. "Hell," he said to himself. "This is going to be a long night."

Checking the time, he saw he'd been sitting there for almost an hour. He spotted the TV remote and picked it up. He flipped it on, found a station playing *It's a Wonderful Life* and watched the last half of it. After it was over, he watched a few other mindless shows until he realized it was almost midnight and turned the TV off. His mind wouldn't still though, and needing to do something, he got up, threw out his empty beer can and grabbed a second one from the fridge. He opened it, took a long gulp, and looked out the window at the backyard. Seeing the shed in the moonlight, he walked closer and stared at it. It sat in the darkness and Rem recalled Chico telling him they would tear it down after the holidays. His memories still flickering, he wanted to go out there, as if being in that shed would in some odd way bring him closer to Jenny.

He turned and spotting a blanket on the couch, he pulled it off and draped it over himself, then grabbed the tiny battery-operated tree and carrying his beer, he left the house, went into the backyard, and opened the door to the shed. It looked nothing like it had before because the only thing left in it was the sofa. Chico had obviously cleaned out the rest before it could be demolished.

Rem set the tree on the floor and turned it on to the lights-only setting, then sat on the sofa and pulled the blanket around him. It was a chilly night, but he was comfortable enough. He drank his beer while his mind wandered to the past and he couldn't help but review his long, almost unbearable year. It was not something he did often, but he'd learned that shutting it out only caused more pain, so he'd given himself occasional permission to reflect, no matter how hard it was.

Thinking how happy he and Jennie had been, he smiled. But his smile vanished when he recalled the awful night of her death. After he'd been notified about the accident, he'd rushed to the hospital only to learn that she hadn't survived.

Gripping his beer, he remembered his agony at the news and how he'd sobbed over her body until Daniels had been left with no choice but to pull him away.

After that horrific day, he'd turned the tears off. Once home, he'd gone on autopilot. Wanting to be strong for Jennie's family and friends, he'd stayed on autopilot throughout the days leading up to and through the funeral. Even while saying the few words he'd wanted to say at her service, he refused to cry. Afterwards, he'd gone into survival mode. Any hint of emotion was stuffed down and he'd buried it, knowing that if it ever emerged, he'd never survive it. The pain would be too much to bear. So he'd dove into work, pulling long hours, and when he was home, he was either drinking or sleeping. He knew everyone was worried, but he didn't care. He was doing everything he could to not fall apart, and the mere thought of Jennie made him tremble with emotion, so he refused to think of her.

Not long after Jennie's death, his uncle had died, and his Aunt Audrey had decided to move into assisted living. She'd asked Rem if he wanted to rent the house from her and he'd jumped at the chance. It would get him out of his apartment where everything he looked at made him think of how much he'd lost. After the funeral, Rem had put all of Jennie's things into boxes and had stacked them in a corner. He didn't want to look at them because it risked chinking the armor he'd so diligently built up around himself. Once in the new house, he'd placed all of the boxes in an upstairs closet. He wanted it out of sight and out of his mind.

He'd lived that way for three months and no matter what anyone told him about needing to grieve, or expressing his emotions or even just drinking less, he ignored it. He knew if he cracked, he would break completely, and nothing would put him back together.

Sitting on the couch in the shed, he watched the tree's bright lights and recalled the day it had all come crashing down. He'd gotten up one morning and was getting ready for work when he'd opened a drawer in his bathroom. Digging for the toothpaste, he'd spotted something else, and he'd pulled it out and froze. It was a tube of Jennie's lipstick. Once past the shock of seeing it, his anger flared, and it had quickly turned to fury. Who had put the lipstick in his drawer? He knew it hadn't been there before. Was it some kind of sick joke? Enraged, he'd yanked the drawer out and had slammed it and all of its contents onto the tiled floor of the bathroom and then he'd put his fist into the mirror. The glass had cracked, but hadn't shattered and that pissed him off even more, but something else had cracked, too. Rem could almost audibly hear it in his body. His rage morphed into a sob. It bubbled up and before he could stop it, another one emerged and then another. Before he knew it, he was on his bathroom floor, curled up in the fetal position, crying his eyes out.

Nothing would stop the unrelenting flow of tears, and he was certain that he would die from grief. The pain was so intense that he wailed and cursed at God and the world for taking her from him.

He'd paid no attention to the time and when his phone rang, it shocked him when he realized he was thirty minutes late for work. He saw on the display that it was Daniels calling but Rem was blubbering too hard to answer, so he'd texted his partner and told him he was sick, wouldn't be in that day and to tell Lozano.

Daniels, of course, had texted back, wanting to know what was wrong. Blurry eyed, Rem could only respond that he was struggling and needed the time. Thankfully, Daniels had left it at that, and Rem went back to his sobbing. He'd stayed on the floor for a while before he had a brief lull. Thinking he was over the worst of it, he'd gotten up to get some water and wash his face, but the moment he'd made it to his sofa, the emotion had returned in spades. The spigot had been turned on, and nothing Rem attempted could turn it off. Once he gave in, the memories of Jennie flashed and swirled in his brain. The shine of her hair, the softness of her skin, the sound of her laugh, her smile, her touch, her eyes. He remembered everything he could about her. He recalled their first date, their first night together, their first weekend trip. Using his phone, he read all of her text messages and looked at every picture of them since the beginning of their relationship and sobbed through all of it. He cried so hard his head throbbed, his eyes swelled, and his chest ached. And each time he thought he was done, his mind and body betrayed him and the slightest thought of her brought all the tears roaring back.

He stayed that way all day until he'd heard a knock on the door. Still in his pajamas and seeing it was after six o'clock, he'd gotten up and looked out the peephole to see Daniels. Trying to pull it together, he opened the door. Daniels stood outside of it, holding a pizza box and a six-pack of soda.

Rem had taken one look at him and lost it again. All the memories of the four of them together assailed him, and he had to hold on to the door frame to stay upright.

Daniels hadn't said a word, but he'd come inside, closed the door, put the pizza and soda down and had come over to Rem and pulled him into a bear hug. Rem had clutched at Daniels like he was his only remaining lifeline and had sobbed into his shoulder. Barely able to catch his breath, he'd wondered where all the tears were coming from and how it was possible to cry so much.

He'd tried to apologize but it only came out as a garble of words even he couldn't translate. Daniels had only told him that it was about time, had guided him to the sofa and sat Rem on it. He'd found a blanket, draped it over Rem's shoulders and, teary-eyed himself, had sat with Rem while he continued to cry.

It was then that Rem entered a new phase of his grief. He blamed himself for Jennie's death. He yelled that he should have been with her that night. If he had, she'd still be alive. The guilt brought on a whole new bout of sobs, and he screamed at God again for being so cruel. Daniels had tried to comfort him, but Rem couldn't even remember what he'd said. Nothing that anyone told him mattered. All he could feel was fury and rage and guilt and sadness and he just wanted it all to end. He missed her so much.

The memories in full swing, Rem sniffed and wiped away a tear. Thinking back on that hard day, he recalled that he'd sobbed for an unknown amount of time while Daniels sat with him before his energy finally waned, the fury diminished, and his tears dried. His body hurt, though, and his eyes were puffy and red, and his stomach was sore from crying.

Daniels had gone into the kitchen then, warmed the pizza and had brought it out. Rem initially refused to eat but Daniels had insisted and after taking the first bite, Rem's hunger kicked in and famished, he ate half of the pizza before almost collapsing from exhaustion.

Before he could fall asleep, though, Daniels had made him get up and guided him into the bedroom where Rem fell into the sheets. He had a brief memory of Daniels pulling the covers over him before he'd closed his eyes and opened them what seemed like moments later. Sunlight brightened the room, and Rem realized it was morning. He'd slept through the entire night and had barely moved an inch. Rolling out of bed, his body still ached, and his head throbbed, but the tightness around his chest had eased and he no longer felt like he had a vise around his ribs.

Seeing his drawer back in place with his items back in it, he figured he had to thank Daniels for that. The mirror was still cracked though, and his fingers were bruised. He'd washed his splotchy face and red eyes with cold water and jumped into a much-needed shower. When he'd emerged, he smelled bacon and eggs and he'd dressed and left his room to find Daniels in the kitchen making breakfast.

Confused and still a little out of it, Rem had wondered why they weren't going into work, and Daniels told him it was Saturday, and they had the day off. Relieved, Rem had fallen into a chair, glad he didn't have to pretend to have his shit together.

After that weekend, he'd learned he could no longer bury his emotions behind a cloud of pain, so each time he felt the grief return and he wasn't home, he'd find a quiet place to go, whether it was the bathroom or his car, and allow himself to cry. After about ten or fifteen minutes, even with his eyes shimmering and his nose red, he'd get back to whatever he was doing. Daniels had gotten used to Rem disappearing, and when it happened at work, Daniels would cover for him.

At first, Rem needed to escape once or twice a day, but then it became once or twice a week, and then once or twice a month.

He'd experienced a couple of other dark moments since where he'd sunk into a deep depression but Daniels, with his keen sense of when Rem required a little help, had been there to pull him out of it. It was part of the reason Rem had asked to be alone for Christmas. His partner had spent enough time these last nine months taking care of him and he figured Daniels needed the time off.

Now, still sitting and reminiscing in the shed, Rem realized he'd made it through December without shedding a tear, but he wasn't going to make it the whole month.

His emotions building, the grief surfacing, and remembering Jenny, he pulled the blanket closer, leaned to his side on the couch and while the lights on the small tree offered his only illumination, he wept.

Chapter Six

Simon followed Gary through the backyard of the house. It was late and the only sound was the rustling of the wind through the leaves on the trees. The house was on a large lot, and they'd done as Egg had suggested – parked in the back driveway accessed by the alley. The back gate had been unlocked, and they'd taken the walkway up to the door. The yard had a swing set, a bricked porch, and a big shed near the edge of the yard.

Gary approached the door and prepared to break the glass with a rock when Simon tried the door and it opened.

Gary frowned but Simon smiled. "You're the one who always tells me to try it first," said Simon. He swung the door wide. "I can't believe they left it unlocked."

"It's our first Christmas gift," said Gary, walking inside. "Somebody stupid enough not to lock their back door."

They entered a breakfast nook and kitchen which opened up into a large living area. The Christmas tree in the corner brightened the room with its twinkling lights.

Simon looked around. "Why are the lights on? The owners aren't supposed to be here."

"It must be on a timer. They didn't deactivate it." Gary approached the tree. "Looks like they left a couple of gifts behind." He squatted and picked one up. "You want to open one?"

Simon had gone straight to the fridge and opened it. He widened his eyes. "Gary, look at this." He grabbed what looked like a plate of ham and set it on the counter.

Gary joined him in the kitchen. "What else is in there?"

Simon pulled out a deeper, wider dish. He pulled off the covering and smelled it. "I think it's a sweet potato casserole."

"Yuck."

Simon made a face at him. "Have you ever had a sweet potato casserole?"

"No. Have you?"

"No, but my friend Art at school told me it's awesome."

"Put it on the counter then."

Simon put the casserole next to the ham.

"Any dessert?"

Simon spotted a small container of milk, a six-pack of beer, cheese slices, eggs, and various other items but nothing that looked like dessert. "No. It might not be in here, though. Check the counter." He opened a drawer in the fridge and spotted some sodas. He pulled two out and closed the fridge.

Gary walked over to an adjacent counter. "Bingo. Look at this." He pulled a pie plate closer and tore off the cellophane covering. "Score. It's apple."

Simon got a whiff of the pie and his mouth watered. "Screw the gifts. Let's eat."

"Damn straight." Gary picked up the pie plate and set it next to the ham and casserole. He pulled open drawers looking for forks and paused. "You think we should look around first?"

Simon found two plates. "You think someone could be here?"

Gary shrugged and found the forks. He gave one to Simon. "Probably not, but it can't hurt to be sure."

Simon eyed the house. There was a hallway off the front room and an upstairs. "I'll look downstairs. You look up."

They set their forks on the counter, and Gary jogged upstairs. Simon followed the hall, passed the dining room on the other side of the kitchen, and found a laundry room and another bedroom. Nobody was there.

Gary appeared at the top of the stairs. "There's three bedrooms up here. I get the big one." He headed back down.

"I don't care where I sleep," said Simon.

They returned to the kitchen. Gary pulled his gun out of his waistband and set it on the counter.

Simon wished his brother had left it behind. "Why'd you have to bring that?"

Gary scowled. "What kind of stupid question is that? We need it in case somebody shows."

"It's Christmas Eve. Egg said these people are out of town. Who's going to show?" Simon grabbed a hunk of ham and put it on his plate.

Gary also grabbed some ham, found a spoon, and loaded some casserole onto his dish. "You never know. It's better to play it safe."

Simon scooped up some casserole, too. "You wouldn't actually shoot someone, would you?"

Gary hesitated. "Depends."

Concerned by his brother's answer, Simon turned toward Gary, holding the spoon for the casserole. "On what?"

"The situation." His plate loaded, Gary picked it up and put it in the microwave. "What do they have to drink around here?"

Simon slid him a soda. "Here."

"Thanks." He waited for the microwave to ding and then he took his plate to the table and sat.

Simon grabbed the other soda, warmed his food, and joined Gary at the table. They wolfed down the leftovers and then got some pie with milk.

"Art's right," said Gary. "That sweet potato stuff is delicious."

Simon wiped his face on his sleeve and smiled. It was the best meal he'd had in as long as he could remember. "Maybe Mom could make it for us."

Gary snorted. "What planet are you from, idiot? Mom's not making us shit. We're lucky to have lunch at school."

Simon pushed back his empty plate, knowing his brother was right. "What do you want to do now?"

Gary finished his milk. "Let's decide what we're taking. We can load the car before the sun comes up and, in the morning, we can eat some more pie and get out of here."

"I saw some eggs in the fridge, too. We could eat those."

"You can have whatever you want." Gary stood, picked up his plate and brought it to the counter. "I guess there's no point in cleaning." He smiled at Simon.

Simon smiled back. Their mother was a stickler about them cleaning up after themselves. She'd told them numerous times she wasn't their maid and if they left a mess, they'd have to clean it, and if they didn't, there'd be hell to pay. He stood and set his own plate on the counter. "Guess not."

"I saw a TV in a box upstairs. We can grab that." Gary pointed toward the big TV in the living room. "That one's too big."

Simon agreed. Egg had been specific about what to take when they'd started burglarizing homes. Gary drove an older model, four-door sedan that his uncle had sold to him for five hundred dollars. Egg liked it because it was clean and didn't stick out. He'd told them that anything that didn't fit in the trunk should stay behind. Driving around with a huge TV in the backseat drew too much suspicion.

They spent the next half hour going through the house. They took a smaller TV from upstairs, along with the one in the box, some jewelry from a cabinet in an upstairs bedroom, a battery-drained tablet and cell phone they'd discovered in a drawer, and a new PlayStation they found in the downstairs bedroom. Pleased with their haul, they stood in the living room and watched the lights blink on the large tree.

"Let's open the gifts," said Gary. He squatted and pulled out the first one. He opened it and found a box of golf balls plus a gift card to a local sports store. The other package contained a popular board game that a whole family could play.

He dropped the board game on the ground. "Just a bunch of junk."

Simon picked it up. "We should take this home. We could play it."

Gary snorted. "That's stupid. That implies we're a family."

"Aren't we?"

Gary stood. "We're robbing a house on Christmas Eve while our mom hangs out with her boyfriend after working all day. What kind of family is that?"

"It's better than nothing."

"Besides," said Gary, kicking aside the ripped gift wrap, "once I'm eighteen and finish high school, I'm outta there."

Simon stilled. "What? Where are you going?"

Gary picked up the gift certificate and sat on the couch. "It's time for me to move on, Squirt."

Simon sat beside him. "What are you going to do?"

Gary shrugged. "Egg and I have talked about it. He understands. He's going to help me out."

Simon's heart sank. "Gary, listen. You can't keep hanging out with that guy."

"Why the hell not?"

"Because he's dangerous. He's not looking out for you. He's using you."

Simon narrowed his eyes. He pulled his gun out that he'd returned to his waistband after eating. "He gave me this and you say he's not looking out for me? He's looking out for both of us. You joined this little party, remember? He didn't have to okay that."

"I only agreed to it because of you. I wanted to be sure you were okay."

Gary gripped the gift card. "Why wouldn't I be okay? And I don't need you looking out for me. I can look out for myself."

Simon tried to think of a way to get through to his brother. Acting like Egg was a friend and relying on him for support was a ticket straight to jail or worse. Simon took a deep breath. "If it wasn't for Trey, you and I both know that you would have never hooked up with Egg."

Gary glared. "You don't know shit, stupid. Trey's got nothing to do with this."

Simon didn't back down. "You know it does. Before Trey, you were going to finish high school and learn a trade, like plumbing or construction. You wanted out but the right way, not this way."

"What's wrong with this way? It's easy money."

"Maybe it is now, but it won't stay that way. You keep working with Egg and the jobs will get riskier."

"They'll also pay more."

"What good is the money if you're sitting in jail?" He pointed at Gary. "Look at you, holding a gun and threatening to shoot it if you need to. You could kill someone and then where would you be? That's not you. And if you think Egg's going to help you out of that mess, you're dead wrong."

Gary huffed and leaned back on the couch. "I know what I'm doing. Unlike you, I'm not stupid. Egg said he'd back me up and he will." He eyed the gift card. "I'm going to give this to him. He might like it." He tucked it into his back pocket.

Simon tried again. "Listen to me. Once you're eighteen, you've got to leave Egg behind."

"And do what? Flip hamburgers?"

"Sure. Why not? We've made some money. Between that and a job, you could make it through trade school in no time."

Gary studied him and chuckled. "I know what this is. You want all the loot for yourself."

Simon dropped his jaw. "What are you talking about?"

"Once I'm out, then you get all of this without having to share. Is that it? You want me gone so you can have it all?" He chuckled again. "I should have known. You always did take after Mom."

Simon couldn't believe his ears. "If it weren't for you, I'd have nothing to do with Egg."

"So now this is all my fault?" He waved at the house. "Look where we are, you jerk. If it weren't for me, we wouldn't be here right now."

"Would that be so bad?"

Gary's face tightened. "You're an ungrateful asshole."

"I'm also your brother, and I'm worried about you."

Gary stood. "Nobody asked you to worry about me. I don't need Mom, you, or anybody."

"You needed Trey, and now he's gone. You blame yourself, and I think you hooked up with Egg because you think you don't deserve any better. But you do."

"Shut up." Gary still held the gun and tightened his hold on it.

Simon stood, too. "After this job, we should stop stealing. Forget Egg. He's not your friend."

"He's a better friend to me than you are."

The words hurt but Simon held strong. "What would Trey think about what you're doing? Would he like it?"

"Trey's dead," screamed Gary. "And he's never coming back. He left me and now I'm on my own. So stop acting like you know me and trying to tell me what to do. You and Mom can suck it." He turned and stomped away. "You can back out of this whenever you want. I don't need you." He headed up the stairs. "I'm going to bed. Sleep wherever you want but stay the hell away from me. We'll leave in the morning after breakfast, go see Egg and then you can go one way and I'll go another."

"Gary, wait."

"Goodnight, jerk." Gary turned the corner at the second floor and disappeared into a bedroom.

Rem blinked and opened his eyes. His vision blurry from sleep, he rubbed his face and groaning, sat up on the sofa. Seeing the small tree that still brightened the small space, he stretched. Obviously, he'd fallen asleep. Checking the time, he saw it was almost six o'clock in the morning. Surprised he'd slept so long, he stood and tried to get the kinks out of his body. Sleeping in that position on the sofa had not done his back any favors. Staring at the tree, the memories swirled again. Sad, but no longer depressed, he squatted, touched one of the branches and thought of Jennie. "I got through last night, Jen. I missed the hell out of you but that's one more challenge out of the way." He rested an elbow on his knee. "And I suspect you were here to see me through it."

One single light blinked from the top of the tree. Surprised, Rem studied it. Was there a setting to blink the lights? He hit the button and the lights went off. He pressed it again, and the music and lights came on. He pressed the button one more time and the music stopped but the lights remained on as before. The tree's lights did not blink and hadn't since he'd turned it on. Assuming it was just a glitch, and he was overthinking it, he smiled. "Now I know I'm tired. I'm starting to believe the tree is communicating." He swiped at his eyes. "Get it together, Remalla."

The single light on the top branch blinked again.

He gaped at it. "What the hell? Since when do you blink?"

The light stayed steady.

Not taking his eyes off the light, his mind raced, and he wondered what was going on. It had to be an electrical issue. Since it was just him in the room, he asked the next question. "Maybe I'm crazy but is someone talking to me?"

The light blinked again.

Warmth traveled through his core and his heart thumped. He swallowed and made the obvious deduction. "Jennie?" he whispered.

The light blinked again.

Emotion bubbled up. He'd heard about this sort of thing before, but it had never happened to him. He'd dreamed of Jennie once or twice, but nothing more obvious than that.

His heart hammering, he held his chest. "Is this really you or am I going crazy?"

The light remained on.

He paused, unsure what to think. "Are you really trying to tell me you're here?"

The light blinked.

"Holy—" Rem fell back on his butt. He sat cross-legged and gawked at the tree. His throat tightened and he didn't care if he was crazy or not. "If that's really you, I miss you. So much."

The light blinked.

Shocked, he clutched his stomach. "I knew you were here. I could feel you. I know I've sensed you around me. I just didn't really buy that it was you."

The light blinked.

Tears blurred his vision. "Thank you for being here." He sniffed. "I love you."

The light blinked.

"I wish you hadn't left."

The light didn't blink.

Rem dropped his head. "I hope you're not trying to tell me it was your time." He looked up.

The light blinked.

He shook his head. "Sorry. But I'm not ready to accept that. I don't think I ever will be."

The light stayed steady.

"I will miss you for the rest of my life."

No blinking.

"You still here?"

A blink.

Rem's breath caught and he fought back tears. "Maybe one day, I'll be able to breathe again whenever I think of you."

A blink.

He smiled softly. "Thanks for the vote of encouragement." He swiped at a watery eye. "I suppose the next thing you're going to tell me is that I'll find love again."

The light blinked.

Rem put his hand over his heart. "I was just kidding." He blotted a tear that trickled down his cheek with his sleeve. "Will you come visit again?"

The light blinked twice.

Rem chuckled. "Wait till I tell Daniels about this. I'll let him know you said hi."

Another blink.

Shaking from the encounter, he talked a few more minutes but the light remained steady. He figured Jennie had said what she'd needed to and had left. Reeling from the encounter, he made himself stand and shake out his nervous energy. He still wasn't sure he believed it but nothing else could explain the interaction.

His heart rate slowing, he decided it was time to leave the shed and face Christmas day. Ready to get back to the house, he pulled the blanket around him, picked up his half empty beer, which had remarkably not spilled while he'd slept, grabbed the miracle tree, and left the shed.

Heading back to the house and feeling better than he had in a long time, he dumped the remains of his beer into the grass, walked up to the back door and opened it. The tree in the living room continued to twinkle, and he set the smaller tree on the breakfast table. He hit the button to turn it off but instead of pushing the button once, he hit it twice and the music started to play. Startled by the sound, he hit the button twice more to turn it and the lights off. The tree went dark and silent, and Rem considered leaving the lights on. What if Jennie wanted to talk again? He quickly deduced that was silly. He couldn't leave the tree on forever and stare at it for the rest of his life. If Jenny found a way to communicate through the tree's lights, she could find another. There were literally lights everywhere. He left the tree on the table, turned, and passed the kitchen on his way to the back bedroom.

Seeing items on the counter and in the sink, he stopped. Perplexed, he walked closer. He stared for a second, completely confused. "What in the hell?" he said. He knew this mess wasn't there when he'd arrived, and he wasn't a sleepwalker. His heart rate ticking up again, he looked into the living room and spotted the board game and box of golf balls he'd bought Chico and his family under the tree, and the wrapping paper in a crumpled ball on the floor.

His mind raced when he realized that someone had paid the house a visit while he'd been asleep in the shed. Despite the quiet, he had to assume that someone could still be there.

Hoping it was just another one of his cousins who'd known Chico was gone and had decided to stop by after having too many drinks, Rem crept toward the bedroom down the hall. He'd left his badge and cell in his knapsack and unfortunately, had left his gun at home. Feeling more and more certain that this was not a random cousin making a late-night stop, he picked up his speed when he realized the music from the tree would have alerted anyone in the house. Rounding the corner, he started down the hall when something hard and small was jabbed into his back.

"Make one move," said a male voice, "and I'll shoot."

Chapter Seven

GARY PRESSED THE GUN into the man's back. His fingers shook and his heart raced, but he'd had no choice but to do something before the man found Simon or called the police. The minute Gary had heard the music, he'd sat upright, jumped out of the bed, grabbed the gun, and raced into the hall. He peered down the stairs and saw the man in the kitchen.

The man eyed the mess Gary and Simon had left in the sink and on the counter. "What in the hell?" he'd said. He was tall with broad shoulders and had long dark hair tucked behind his ears. Gary had to assume the owner had come home. Acting fast, he moved quietly but swiftly down the stairs before the man left the kitchen. He was glad the stairs were carpeted because it muted his footfalls.

He darted into the dining room and squatted low so he couldn't be seen. After his argument with Simon, Gary hadn't slept well, and he'd crept down in the night to check on his brother. He'd found him in the back bedroom, fast asleep. If the man found Simon, that would be it. Gary had to stop him first before the element of surprise was lost.

Just as he feared, the man came around the corner and started down the hall toward Simon's room, and Gary had no choice but to jump out and jab the gun into the man's back. He told him not to move or he'd shoot. The man froze and held his hands out.

Standing there, Gary had no idea what to do next. He cursed at himself when he realized he hadn't worn his mask. If this man saw him or Simon, he could identify them. "Move," he said. "Back into the kitchen." He pressed the gun harder into the man's back.

"Take it easy," said the man. "No need to get violent." He turned his head. "Was it you who helped yourself to the food?"

Gary was glad it was dark so the man couldn't get a good look at him. "I said, move into the kitchen." He had to get him out of the hall before Simon heard the noise and woke up.

"Okay. I'm going." He turned back, rounded the corner, and stepped into the kitchen. "Now what?"

Gary thought the man seemed oddly at ease for someone with a gun on him. "Go to the table."

"Listen," said the man. "I've got no beef with you. You were hungry and you opened the gifts under the tree. No big deal. It's Christmas. Why don't we call it even and you can go. No harm done."

Confused and scared, Gary tried to think. He had to get Simon out of there and preferably without this guy seeing him. He wondered what Egg would do. "Sit in the chair and face the wall."

The man didn't move.

"Now," he said louder. He had to show this guy he meant business. He jabbed the gun again.

The man took a step. "How old are you?"

Gary didn't like that question. "Shut up," he said. "Sit or I will shoot you."

"All right. I'm going." The man walked slowly toward the table.

Gary started to feel a little more confident. If he could get this guy in a seat, maybe he could tie him up and he and Simon could get out of there without too much damage done. He looked around for anything to use as a binding. The house was still dark though, and if he turned on the light, the man would easily see him.

"You know, if you shoot me, you're staring at a lot of jail time."

"Stop talking." Gary followed the man to the table, still debating what to do. Maybe he could hit the guy over the head and knock him out cold? He'd never done that before and wondered how hard he'd have to hit him.

"There are ways out of this, kid."

The word 'kid' pissed Gary off, and he raised his gun to hit the man in the head when the lights came on in the kitchen. The man squinted and Gary didn't waver but jabbed the gun harder into his back. "Don't move."

Simon stood in the doorway, his hair askew. His eyes widened. "Gary, what the hell are you doing?"

Gary cursed.

"Gary, huh?" asked the man. He glanced back, getting a good look at Gary. "Nice to meet you. I'm Rem."

ele

Rem eyed the kid in the doorway. He couldn't have been older than sixteen and something told him the one with the gun was close to the same age. They also looked similar. Putting the pieces together, he realized he'd interrupted the burglars he and Daniels had been investigating for the last six weeks. He couldn't believe they were so young.

"You two brothers?" asked Rem.

Neither answered so Rem took that as a yes. "What's your name?" he asked the one who'd turned on the light.

"Shut up," said Gary.

"Simon," said the kid.

Gary cursed again. "Stop talking, you idiot."

"Gary and Simon," said Rem. "Shouldn't you two be home waiting for Santa's arrival?"

The gun pressed harder into his back, and he winced. He was going to have a nice bruise when this was over.

"Sit the hell down," said Gary.

Rem did as he was asked and sat at the breakfast table. Gary kept the gun on him, and Rem kept his hands visible.

"Gary, don't do this." Simon walked further into the kitchen.

Gary raised his voice and glared at Rem. "Who are you? Why are you here?"

Rem wondered how to answer. He didn't know what these kids did or didn't know. He decided to stick to the truth. "My cousin lives here. I'm staying the night." He chuckled at the irony of the situation. "To protect it from burglars."

"Well, you suck at it," said Gary.

"Apparently," said Rem.

"Gary, leave him alone," said Simon.

"I can't leave him alone," shouted Gary. "He knows our names. He's seen us."

"He knows our first names," said Simon. "And who cares if he saw us?" He stepped closer. "The stuff is in the car. Let's just lock him in a room and get out of here."

Rem waited to hear what Gary would say.

Gary remained quiet before he finally spoke. "Where're your things?" he asked Rem.

Rem raised a brow. "My things?"

"Yeah," said Gary. "If you were going to sleep here tonight, you've got a bag or something. Where is it?"

Rem didn't want to answer. If they found his knapsack, they'd discover his badge. "It's upstairs."

"Where upstairs?"

Simon got closer to Rem and stared at him. His face fell. "Oh, no."

"What's the matter?" asked Gary.

"He's lying. His stuff's in the back room."

"What are you talking about?" asked Gary.

Simon looked at his brother. "Before I went to sleep, I looked around. I found a bag in the closet. There was an identification with a badge inside it. It has his picture on it." He paused. "He's a cop, Gary."

"Shit," said Gary.

Rem sighed and slumped in his seat.

Gary's face lost its color. "Shit. Shit. Shit."

Rem figured he ought to say something. "Take it easy. It's not that big of a deal."

"Shut up," said Gary. He spoke to Simon. "Go get his stuff. Bring it here."

Simon ran out of the kitchen. He was back a few seconds later with Rem's knapsack and the bag with the other gifts in it. Simon dug through the knapsack and pulled out the badge. "Here." He showed it to Gary.

Gary studied it. "Hell. He's a detective."

Simon took the badge back and returned it to the knapsack.

"Is there a gun?" asked Gary.

"No," said Simon. "Not in the bag."

"No gun," said Rem. "I didn't bring one."

"Stand up," said Gary. "Check him, Si. Make sure he doesn't have a weapon."

"Are you serious?" asked Simon.

Rem stood and raised his hands. "It's okay, Simon. Check away. I'm not carrying."

Simon eyed him tentatively and moved closer. He patted Rem's pockets and waist and even his ankles. Rem was impressed at his thoroughness. "Nice job." He sat down again.

"I watch a lot of cop shows," said Simon. He stepped back toward his brother. "Now what do you want to do?"

Gary ran his free hand through his messy hair. "I don't know." He expelled a long breath. "I should call Egg, but it's too early."

Rem made a mental note of the name Egg.

"C'mon," said Simon. "Let's just get out of here."

Gary's face tightened. "He's a cop, you idiot. The minute we leave, he's on the phone with his cop friends. He'll describe our faces and tell our names."

"So what?" asked Simon. "You know what Egg said. If we're caught, we'll go to Juvie. No big deal."

"I don't want to go to Juvie, do you? Besides, if we get caught, Egg will dump us. He'll say we're too hot, and then what do we do?"

"Let him dump us. I don't care. We don't need him."

"Just shut up," yelled Gary, glowering. "I have to think. Keep an eye on him," he said to Simon. He aimed the weapon at Rem's head. "You move and you die."

Rem put his hands back on the table. "Message received. I'll stay right here." Rem had sensed more than one opportunity to get out of this mess. He could have taken the gun from Gary when the lights came on or when Simon had come closer to check for a weapon. He'd held back though because the risk wasn't zero that Gary could pull the trigger just from the stress and tension alone. He didn't think Gary would intentionally shoot him; he was just a scared kid who didn't know what to do. Thinking it through, he figured his best shot was to talk them down. If he could convince them to see that their life wasn't over if they were caught, he might get them to surrender. Taking a quiet breath, he stayed calm and hoped that would help keep them calm, too. "I'm not going to try anything," he added, trying to instill some trust.

Simon sat in a chair on the opposite side of the table. "I'll watch him."

Gary backed away but still held the gun. His face expressed a gamut of emotions. "We should tie him up."

"With what?" asked Simon.

"I don't know. Look around."

Simon got up and checked the kitchen. "There's nothing here."

Rem checked the clock on the wall. It was still early, but the sun was coming up on a pretty Christmas morning. Of all the problems he'd expected to face that day, being held hostage by two teenagers was not one of them. He squirmed in his chair. "Before you do that, I'm going to need to use the facilities."

Simon looked up from his search.

Rem scrunched his face. "I had two beers last night, fell asleep in the shed, and just woke up. If I don't use the restroom, that mess in the sink is the least of your troubles."

The brothers made eye contact.

"I promise I'll behave," said Rem, raising his hands.

"Go check the bathroom," said Gary to Simon. "Make sure there's nothing he can use as a weapon in there."

Simon ran out to check the guest bathroom off the hallway.

"What? You think I'm going to spray you with hairspray or hit you with a toilet brush?" asked Rem.

Simon returned. "There's nothing in there."

"Get up," said Gary.

"Thank you." Rem stood and walked slowly to the hall and into the bathroom with Gary behind him, holding the gun on him.

Simon followed Gary and Rem walked into the bathroom. He started to shut the door.

"Leave it cracked," said Gary.

Rem didn't argue. If he was going to get these two to trust him, he'd do what they wanted. "Sure thing." He left the door cracked, used the restroom, flushed, and washed his hands. He reached for a towel that hung on a rack over the toilet, and inadvertently knocked over a small vase with fake flowers in it. The vase hit the ground with a loud clatter and broke. Gary rushed in and Rem froze when Gary, his hands shaking, aimed the gun at Rem's face.

Chapter Eight

DANIELS ROLLED TO HIS side and snuggled around Marjorie. She stirred and wiggled closer to him. "You awake?" she asked.

He smelled her strawberry-scented hair. "I am."

"Merry Christmas," she said.

"Merry Christmas."

She trailed her fingers down his forearm. "You get some sleep?"

Daniels smiled. "Once we finally had the chance." He nuzzled her neck, thinking he could never get enough of her.

She sighed with satisfaction. "That was a fun Christmas Eve." She rolled toward him and cupped his cheek. "Santa was very, very good to me."

Daniels' heart skipped. "Santa aims to please." He moved his arm around her and stroked her back.

She held his gaze. "You sure you had a good time at my mom's?"

"Of course I did. It was great. I especially loved the orange oven mitts she gave me."

Marjorie chuckled. "The cat pictures all over them were a nice touch."

"It made me think of something Rem would give me."

She lowered her hand to his chest. "You were thinking about him last night, weren't you?"

Daniels lifted his head and rested it on his hand. "Was it that obvious?"

"Didn't have to be. I was thinking about him, too. You think he did okay last night?"

Daniels wondered the same. "I don't know. I talked to him before he went over to Chico's and he seemed fine, although he wouldn't admit Chico was out of town. I know Rem, though. If something's bugging him, he'll keep it to himself for as long as he can before he admits to it."

"Maybe it was good for him to be alone. It lets him grieve in privacy. That's understandable, especially now at Christmas."

"Privacy is one thing, but loneliness is another. Loneliness leads to depression, and he's had more than a few bouts of that this year."

"You told him to call you if he needed anything."

"I did, but he knows we had plans, and he wouldn't have interrupted." He eyed the time. "I wonder if he's up yet."

"You still plan on going over there this morning, even though he's coming to dinner tonight?"

"Definitely. I can only let him hide for so long. I'll take him his gift and a cup of coffee, plus some of those cinnamon poppers you made. He'll love 'em." He stroked her hip. "In fact, maybe I'll surprise him. Just show up so he can't bitch about me coming over."

"That's a good idea." She shifted her head on the pillow. "I'm glad you're going. It will make me feel better, too."

Daniels lifted his hand and ran his fingers through her blonde hair. "It will, huh?"

"Yes." She caressed his chest with her fingers.

"Anything else you can think of that might make you feel better?" He grinned at her.

She snuggled closer and grinned back. "I don't know. What did Santa have in mind?"

He leaned in and kissed her nose, then trailed more kisses down her cheek to her neck, where he nibbled her soft skin. "I think Santa has a few more tricks up his sleeve." He ran his hand down her body and heard her suck in a breath. "I hear you've been very good this year." He moved his hand lower, and she moaned.

"Oh, Santa," she said breathless, "you're so bad."

Pleased at her reaction, Daniels raised his lips to hers and captured them with a hungry kiss.

Rem sat in the chair at the breakfast table. His stomach rumbled, and he checked the clock on the wall. He'd been sitting there close to two hours. Simon sat across the table from him, and Gary paced in the living room. He'd made a few phone calls with no luck. No one had answered. Now he seemed to be biding his time until he got in touch with the mysterious Egg.

After the incident in the bathroom, Rem had managed to calm Gary down enough to realize the vase had been knocked over by mistake and he wasn't trying to escape. Gary had eased up, and Simon had walked Rem back to the kitchen where he'd been sitting ever since. They'd made no mention of tying him up again, and Rem didn't remind them.

He'd stayed quiet, hoping Gary would relax and realize the best way out was to either leave Rem behind and take off, or surrender, but watching Gary pace with anxiety, he began to wonder if he was assuming too much. Deciding he needed more information, he struck up a conversation with Simon. "So, since we seem to be hanging out, why don't we get to know each other. How'd you two end up robbing houses?"

Simon glanced at Gary, who continued to pace. "It seemed easy enough, plus we make money."

Rem thought about the timings of the burglaries. "How'd you pull it off? Aren't you two in school and at home at a decent hour?"

Simon shrugged. "Gary and I have decent grades. We ditch school every now and then and nobody cares. And our mom's not usually home until later." He set his elbow on the table. "And when school let out for the holiday, we had plenty of free time."

"You two are pretty good at it. Did somebody teach you?"

Simon averted his eyes.

"Was it this Egg person?"

Simon shrugged again.

Rem nodded. "Why Christmas Eve? Where's your mom or dad?"

Simon scratched at something on the tabletop. "Mom works two jobs. Dad took off when we were kids. Mom spent Christmas Eve with her boyfriend. We'll see her later today." He paused. "I hope."

Rem wasn't sure he heard right. "Your mom spent last night with her boyfriend and not you?" He found it hard to believe. "What about gifts? When do you open them?"

"No gifts. She can't afford them."

"But you said she's working two jobs."

Simon shifted in his seat. "I know. But it's still not enough. Birthdays and Christmas are luxuries we can't afford."

Rem sat up. "Birthdays, too?" He couldn't imagine abandoning kids on Christmas Eve and not giving them gifts for either the holiday or their birthday.

Simon pursed his lips and kept scratching at the table. "It's fine."

"No. Actually, it's not. It's pretty crappy."

He straightened. "She's doing her best."

Rem understood Simon's need to protect his mother. Most kids did despite how badly they were being raised. "That's why you came here last night?"

Simon nodded. "Egg said—" He froze, realizing he'd just used Egg's name, which Gary didn't like. "We were told the house would be empty for a few days, and we could take our time."

Rem leaned back in his chair. "Sorry I interrupted your plans."

"Me, too." He stopped picking at the table. "You like being a cop?"

Pleased Simon was opening up to him, he considered the question. "It has its ups and downs, like any job."

"But you catch the bad guys?"

"Sometimes. We try our best, but we don't always succeed."

Simon went quiet for a moment. "What's going to happen to us if we get caught?"

Rem debated how to answer. He noted Gary had stopped pacing and suspected he was listening. "Depends. You give yourselves up without any resistance and it will go a lot easier on you. But if you don't, it could be a problem. Right now, you've just broken into a few homes, and thankfully, no one's been hurt."

"Will we go to juvie?"

"Based on your age, Simon, yes, you will. If you're convicted, your record will be cleared when you turn eighteen."

Simon blew out a breath.

"That's so long as no one gets hurt." He eyed Gary. "How old is your brother?"

"Seventeen."

Rem pointed. "As long as he doesn't fire that weapon, he might be okay."

Gary looked over. "What do you mean?"

"You shoot somebody with that, and they'll try you as an adult. And then it'll be a long time before you see the sun again."

Gary's face furrowed. "That's a lie. Egg told me as long as I was under eighteen, it won't be held against me no matter what I did."

"Well, I hate to be the bearer of bad news," said Rem, "but your friend Egg lied to you. They've tried kids younger than you as adults. It's not that uncommon. But, if you surrender peacefully, agree to turn in this Egg, who I'm guessing is the ringleader in a multitude of crimes, they'll go easy on you."

Simon looked at Gary with wide eyes. "Maybe we should consider that."

Gary snickered. "He's lying to us, idiot. Can't you see that? He just wants us to give up Egg. It's a win-win for him. But I'm not buying his bullshit."

Simon crossed his arms. "I don't think he's lying."

Gary scowled at his brother. "Then when it comes time to leave, you can stay with him for all I care."

"I don't want to stay with him," said Simon. "I want to stay with you."

"Then shut the hell up and do what I say," yelled Gary. "You got that?"

"I just don't want you to go to jail," said Simon.

"Don't worry." Gary aimed a pointed stare at Rem. "I am not going to jail."

Rem shook his head. "I'm not trying to hurt you, kid. I'm trying to help you."

"Stop calling me 'kid,'" shouted Gary.

Rem raised his hands. "Sorry...Gary." He paused. "And rest easy, because if you stay on this path, juvenile court won't call you a kid either. And once you turn eighteen, no court is ever going to call you a kid."

Gary straightened his aim. "I could shoot you right now."

Simon stood. "Gary, don't."

Rem tried his best to remain relaxed. "You do that, you'll go to prison." He nodded toward Simon. "And your brother would be considered an accessory. They might even try him as an adult, too."

Simon dropped his jaw.

Gary didn't back down. "They'd have to catch us first."

Rem didn't respond. His plan wasn't to antagonize Gary, but it seemed to be all he was doing. "I'm not trying to frighten you. I'm just being honest. You make the right choices, and you can still walk away from this with options. Don't destroy that because you're scared."

"I'm not scared," yelled Gary.

Rem noted Gary's trembling hand. "There's nothing wrong with being scared. I'm scared right now. I bet Simon is, too."

Simon bobbed his head up and down.

Rem softened his voice. "Just take some deep breaths, ki—I mean Gary. That's what I'm doing."

Gary seemed to calm when his phone rang. He jumped, and Rem tensed when he feared Gary would pull the trigger out of sheer nerves. Thankfully, the gun didn't go off and Gary pulled his cell out and answered. "Hey," he said. He lowered the gun, resumed his pacing, and spoke quietly into the phone.

Rem exhaled and tried to slow his thumping heart.

"My brother isn't a bad guy," said Simon, returning to his seat. He watched Gary pace. "He's just had some hard times."

"That's life, Simon. Everyone has hard times." Simon went quiet and Rem sensed an opportunity to understand Gary better. "What kind of hard times?"

Simon studied his fingers as if contemplating whether to answer. He shifted to face Rem. "Our cousin Trey was murdered six months ago."

Rem rested his elbows on the table. "I'm sorry to hear that. Were you all close?"

"We were, but Trey and Gary especially. They were the same age, and they were best friends. They did everything together."

"What happened?"

Simon hesitated. "Trey was a good kid. So was Gary until Trey died. They both worked at Showburger. Trey's dad owns it, and it was Trey's and Gary's first job. Trey saved up enough money to get his dad a watch for his birthday. Gary had seen it in a store window and had suggested that Trey's dad would like it. So, Trey bought it and gave it to his dad, but a month later, Trey's dad was mugged, and the watch was stolen. They beat up his dad pretty good, too. Trey had asked around and told Gary he'd learned who was responsible." Simon went back to studying his hands. "We live in a neighborhood where the bad guys get away with stuff because everyone's afraid of them."

Rem understood that kind of neighborhood. He'd lived in a few himself.

"Gary told Trey to leave it alone, but Trey wouldn't listen. Said he was going to get the watch back for his dad. He disappeared after work one day and the day after that, they found his body in a park across from the school. He'd been shot in the head."

Rem's heart sunk. "That's horrible." He recalled a murder case of a teenager his fellow Detectives Georgios and Titus had been investigating about six months back. "What's Trey's last name?"

"McDermott."

The name rang a bell. Georgios and Titus had investigated but no one in the neighborhood would talk, and the case remained open and unsolved.

Simon slumped in his seat. "The cops came and talked to us, and Gary told them about the watch and what Trey was going to do, but he didn't know more than that." He eyed his brother who still spoke on the phone. "Gary hasn't been the same since. He blames himself for Trey's death, but it wasn't his fault."

"No. It wasn't." Rem marveled over the parallels between him and Gary. They were both grieving loved ones, blaming themselves and suffering with how to cope in a world where the person you loved was no longer in it. "But I get it. It takes time to move past something so difficult. Especially when you feel your guts have just been yanked out of you."

Simon studied him. "You sound like you understand."

Rem nodded. "I lost my girlfriend nine months ago. She was hit by a drunk driver on her way home, on a night when I was supposed to be with her, but I got busy at work." The familiar grief reared up. "And I've struggled with forgiving myself, so I understand the anger and pain. It can mess with your head."

Simon went back to scratching the table. "Well, at least you didn't start robbing houses."

Rem couldn't help but smile. "No. I didn't. But I had my other vices." He thought of Daniels. "Thankfully, I have a friend who's been helping me through it."

Simon pursed his lips. "Gary's friend was Trey."

"He's got you though, doesn't he?" He spoke to Simon but kept an eye on Gary who was still on his phone. "No matter how mad he gets, it's pretty obvious he cares about you."

"I annoy him more than anything."

"You're still his brother and no matter what he says or does, he'll protect you."

Simon shook his head. "You don't know Gary very well."

"I know him better than you think." He thought of his own youth and the grudges he'd carried and how it had taken time to make peace with his father's failures. "If it hadn't been for my mom, I could have easily taken the path Gary is on."

"I'm on the same path."

Rem tipped his head. "Do you want to be on it? Something tells me the only reason you're here is because of your brother. You want to protect him, too."

Simon set his jaw. "I'm not doing a very good job."

Seeing the worry on Simon's face, Rem determined to find a way out of this. If he didn't and Gary ended up in prison for either murder or attempted murder, Simon would be yet another victim in the guilt game and could end up on the same road as his brother. "I think you're doing just fine. You may have strayed off the path a bit further than you needed to, but there's still hope. We just need to get Gary to see that."

Simon started to answer when Gary's voice raised. "No," he said into his cell. "I need to talk to him. He needs to tell me what to do. Not you." He eyed Rem with angst-filled eyes and then winced. "Fine," he answered into the phone. "I'll take care of it." His voice shaking, he hung up and put the phone in his back pocket. He raised the gun toward Rem.

"Who was that?" asked Simon.

"Doesn't matter," answered Gary.

Rem didn't like the look in Gary's eyes. "Was it Egg? He tell you what to do?" Gary shook his head.

"It was Buzzard, wasn't it?" asked Simon.

Rem sat up. "Who's Buzzard?"

"Sort of Egg's right-hand man," said Simon. "I don't like him. He scares me." Gary didn't say a word but continued to aim the gun.

"What did Buzzard tell you to do?" asked Rem.

Gary's face had paled, and he looked sick. "Go in the other room, Simon."

Simon's face dropped. "What are you doing?"

"I said go in the other room."

Simon stood and walked over to him. "You can't shoot him. That's a death sentence and you know it. He's a cop."

Rem slowly raised a hand and soothed his voice. "Listen to your brother, Gary. He's right." His own fingers shook. No matter how crappy his year had been, he didn't want it to end like this.

"Please, Gary." Simon walked closer. "Don't do it."

Rigid, Gary never took his eyes off Rem. "I have to. If I don't…"

"Forget what they told you," said Simon. "You already know the right thing to do."

Gary didn't waver. "Buzzard's right. If I expect to get any respect from Egg, I have to take care of my own problems."

"This isn't taking care of your problems," said Rem. "This is only adding to them. You're taking care of *their* problems. And when you're caught, they won't lift a finger to help you. They aren't your friends, Gary." He stayed calm but his heart rate had surged.

"You don't know what you're talking about," said Gary.

"Yes, he does," said Simon. "He wants to help us."

Gary sneered. "He's gaslighting you. He's just telling you what you want to hear. If I didn't have this gun, we'd be in jail, and he'd be enjoying a big Christmas meal today. He doesn't give a shit about us."

"That's not true," said Simon.

"Shut up, Simon, and leave the damn room," yelled Gary. He spoke to Rem. "Stand up."

Simon shook his head. "No. I won't. I can't let you do this." He pulled on Gary's free hand. "What would Trey think? He'd never want this for you. He was your friend. Not Egg and not Buzzard."

"Leave Trey out of this," yelled Gary.

"I won't," yelled Simon, "because you know I'm right."

Praying for a solution to get Gary to see reason, Rem stood. He wasn't anywhere near Gary to be able to tackle him and take the gun, but he hoped if he kept talking, he could get closer. "I heard about Trey. You two were tight, weren't you?"

Gary cursed and screamed at Simon. "You told him about Trey?"

"Don't get mad at Simon," said Rem. "He's scared and worried about you." He took a small step closer. "And I bet he's right about Trey. Trey was your best friend. If he loved you, he wouldn't want you to do this."

Gary jabbed the gun toward Rem. "You don't know shit about Trey, so shut up."

Rem kept his hands up. "No, I didn't know Trey, but I know a little about grief and guilt and what it can do to you."

Gary's eyes shimmered. "Shut up. You're lying."

"He's not lying," said Simon. "He lost someone, too. His girlfriend. Not long before Trey. A drunk driver hit her."

Gary bit his lip. "That's not true. I don't believe you."

"It's true," said Rem. "Her name was Jennie. And if she hadn't died, I would have married and had kids with her. I had my whole future planned, but fate took it away."

Gary hardened his gaze.

"Why do you think I was here alone on Christmas Eve? Why am I here today?" Rem took another small step. "I didn't want to be with anyone. Jennie loved this time of year and spending last Christmas with her was one of the best times of my life. I miss her every day, like you must miss Trey."

"I don't want to talk about Trey," said Gary.

Rem set his hand on the kitchen counter. "I get it. I didn't want to talk about Jennie for a long time, until I couldn't help it anymore, and it all hit me at once." He took a risk and probed a little deeper. "What about you? Do you talk about Trey? Have you cried over his loss?"

Gary glared. "I told you I don't want to talk about it. He's gone and he's not coming back."

"He's right, Gary. You don't like to talk about him," said Simon. "You get mad every time I mention him."

Rem thought of the blinking light on the Christmas tree that morning. "And this may come as a surprise to you, but he's not really gone. Physically, you can't see him, but he's around and I bet he tries to communicate with you. Do you sometimes sense him, like he's near but you just ignore it?" He prayed this conversation would pull Gary off the ledge and help him do the right thing.

"Do you think I'm stupid?" asked Gary, scowling. "You think Trey's ghost is walking around trying to talk to me? What are you? One of those weirdos who speaks to the dead?" He pulled his arm out of Simon's grip. "I can't believe you're listening to this guy, Si. He's insane."

Rem took another step. "I'm not insane. I know what I'm talking about." He eyed the small tree that still sat on the table. "Turn that tree on and maybe you'll see what I mean." He knew it was a long shot that the light would blink as it had before, but he had to try and distract Gary.

Simon glanced at the tree. "What does the tree have to do with it?"

"Turn it on and I'll show you." Rem gestured toward the small tree. Even if the light didn't blink, it might buy him some time.

Simon hesitated but walked toward the table. "Are you serious?" Gary asked Simon. "You're going to do it?"

"It's a stupid tree," said Simon. "What can it hurt?"

Rem suspected Simon was willing to try anything to keep Gary from doing something stupid. Simon reached for the tree.

"There's a button on the side," said Rem. "Hit it twice."

Simon picked it up. He hit the button and the music played, and the lights illuminated. Simon hit it again and the music turned off, but the lights remained on. "Now what?"

"Put it on the counter." Rem hoped Jennie or Trey was listening or this was going to be a failed experiment that could cost him his life.

Simon set the tree on the kitchen counter.

"This is dumb," said Gary. "You're just wasting time and trying to stall."

"Just wait," said Simon. He looked at Rem. "What's supposed to happen?"

"See the lights and how they don't blink?" asked Rem.

Simon nodded.

"This morning, when I was in the shed, the top light blinked." Gary scoffed and Rem knew how it sounded. "I was talking to Jennie and the light would go on and off."

Both boys stared at him with blank expressions. Gary glared again. "He's screwing with us."

"I'm not," said Rem.

"You think it will blink if we ask a question?" asked Simon.

Rem gave silent thanks that Simon was willing to consider it. If he hadn't, he didn't know where he would be right now. "That's what I'm saying."

Gary narrowed his eyes. "This is total bullshit."

"Why not try it?" asked Simon.

"Exactly," said Rem. "If Trey's around right now, I bet he'd want you to know."

"Trey is dead," yelled Gary. "He's not here. He's not talking to me, and he never will again."

"I say we try," said Simon.

Gary snickered again and studied Rem. "Fine. I'll make you a deal. That light flickers, and I won't kill you, but if it doesn't..." He held Rem's gaze.

Rem hesitated. "I'm not sure I'm willing to go that far. How about you don't kill me at all."

Gary tightened his hold on the gun, and Rem wondered how he'd gotten himself into such a crazy situation – relying on a blinking light to save his life.

Gary spoke softly but with force. "If you want to live, then you better pray it blinks."

Simon swiveled toward Gary. "Would you please calm down and think this through?"

Gary bobbed the gun. "Go ahead. Ask it a question, Si."

Simon turned back toward the tree. He seemed uncertain but then spoke. "Is...uhm...anyone here?" He waited, but the light remained steady. "Blink the light if you can."

Nothing happened.

Simon tried again. "Trey? Are you here? If you are, we really need to hear from you. Gary's in a crisis and he needs you."

Rem stared at the light, willing it to blink, but it didn't. "Try again."

"I told you," said Gary. "He's messing with us."

"Trey," said Simon. "This is really important."

Please, Trey, Rem thought to himself. *Blink the light.* He thought of Jennie. *Jennie, if you're here, I could really use your help.* The light didn't blink.

"C'mon, Trey," said Simon.

"That's enough," said Gary. "The cop's lying."

"I'm not lying," said Rem.

"Well, then Trey and your girl have better things to do. They didn't show, just like I said. There are no messages from the dead, and your time's up." Gary took a step closer. "I'm going to tell you one last time, Simon. Leave the room."

"No, I won't," said Simon. "Don't shoot him, Gary."

Gary shifted on his feet. Doubt crossed his features but then he seemed to make up his mind. "Suit yourself." He tensed and Rem wondered if he would actually pull the trigger. He'd doubted it at first but now he wasn't so sure.

Starting to sweat, Rem held still. Simon begged his brother to stop, and then the doorbell rang.

Chapter Nine

NOBODY SAID A WORD, but they all glanced toward the front room. Gary kept the gun on Rem, but he cursed and whispered. "Who the hell is that?"

Grateful for the interruption, Rem wondered the same thing. Maybe one of Chico's friends? A neighbor? "I'm not sure. Maybe somebody my cousin knows."

"This time of the morning? On Christmas Day?" asked Gary.

Rem shrugged. "My cousin knows weird people."

Indecision clouded Gary's features. "Si, go check the peephole."

Simon, his eyes wide, took quiet steps toward the door.

Rem didn't know what to think. Should he try to alert whoever was there to his presence and risk more lives in the process or keep his mouth shut and potentially get shot in the next few minutes? Neither option was great.

Simon returned. "It's a tall blond guy holding something."

Rem frowned just as the knock came again and a voice traveled from outside. "C'mon, Rem. I know you're in there. Your car's outside. Get your lazy butt up and come get your gift."

Rem cursed to himself. It was Daniels.

"Who is that?" asked Gary.

Rem stammered. "Uhm...well...it's my friend."

"Your friend?" asked Simon.

Rem nodded. "He's checking in on me. It is Christmas morning, in case you two forgot."

"Shit," said Gary. "Is he a cop, too?"

Rem chose to be honest. "He's my partner."

The knock came again. "Rise and shine."

Tense, Gary watched the door.

"He's not going anywhere," said Rem.

Gary waved the gun at Rem with a dour expression. "Answer it and get rid of him. He comes in here and you both die." Holding the gun on Rem, he headed toward the front. "Come with me, Si."

Simon followed Gary until they were standing behind the door. Rem walked up to it, wondering what he was going to say. Should he try and warn Daniels? In the past, they'd discussed certain words to use in case one of them was in trouble but if Rem warned Daniels, Daniels would call in the whole damn squad. Rem wasn't sure if that was the best response for this situation and certainly not for Gary and Simon. No matter how tenuous Gary's state of mind was, Rem was holding out hope that he could get himself and Gary and Simon out of this mess with minimal damage.

Daniels knocked again. "You know I'm not leaving until you—"

Rem opened the door. Daniels stood on the porch looking relaxed in jeans and a t-shirt, with a bag hooked over his wrist, holding a plate of something in one hand and a coffee in another. "There you are," he said. "Merry Christmas."

Seeing the coffee, he was halfway tempted to let Daniels in just for that alone. "Merry Christmas."

"Now don't get mad. I know I'm popping in and probably woke you." He looked Rem over. "Were you already up?"

Rem looked down at his wrinkled clothes. "Yeah."

Daniels studied him. "Did you sleep last night?"

"A little. Listen—"

Before he could say anything, Daniels walked up to the door. "I know you're going to say you're fine, but I'm on to you, partner. I bumped into Chico yesterday morning. I know he went out of town, and you were by yourself last night. That's fine, but your period of solitude is over." He raised the plate. "I brought you some of Marjorie's cinnamon poppers and a coffee. Christmas Eve may have been rough, but Christmas morning doesn't have to be."

Rem wanted to groan. "I think that ship has sailed."

Daniels furrowed his brow. "What?"

"Nothing. Listen. Thanks so much for everything, but I'm really fine. I...uh...I'm liking my quiet time. Why don't you—"

"Nonsense. I know what you're doing. If you really want me out of your hair, then at least let me drop off my gift. I won't stay long."

"No, really. I think—" Rem was standing to the side of the door and Daniels walked up and pushed past him.

"I'm not taking no for an answer, buddy." He entered the house.

Rem grabbed his arm. "Wait. Maybe we should—" He tried to pull Daniels back, but his partner wouldn't budge. Gary stepped out with the gun and kicked the door shut with his foot.

He aimed the gun at Daniels who dropped his jaw. "What in the—"

"Merry Christmas," said Gary.

"Who are you?" asked Daniels. He eyed Simon who stood beside Gary. "Who are they?"

Rem sighed. "Santa left me an unexpected gift."

"You weren't *that* bad this year, were you?" asked Daniels.

Rem waved a hand. "Meet our friendly neighborhood robbers."

Daniels studied the brothers. "You've got be kidding."

Gary straightened his aim. "Do we look like a joke?"

"No. Certainly not." He shot a look at Rem. "How come you didn't use our warning system?

Rem rolled his eyes. "You didn't exactly give me a chance."

Daniels gestured at Rem with the coffee. "How hard is it? You just say something right out of the gate."

"Don't you think that would have sounded a little suspicious? Besides, I had a gun on me. I was a little distracted."

"Since when do you have a problem working under pressure?"

Rem blew out a frustrated breath.

"Would you two shut up," yelled Gary. "Si, search him. Make sure he doesn't have a gun."

Daniels frowned at Gary. "Does it look like I have a weapon?"

"Just humor him," said Rem.

Simon moved closer to Daniels, and Daniels raised his arms. Simon checked his pockets, waist, and ankles. "He's okay," said Simon. He opened the bag. "It's just a package."

Daniels lowered his arms. "I can't believe this is happening."

"Join the club," said Rem.

"Move," said Gary. "Back into the kitchen."

Daniels looked into the house. "I'm assuming it's this way?"

"C'mon," said Rem. "You can keep me company."

Daniels started toward the kitchen. "How long have they been holding you here?"

"All morning," said Rem. "We've been getting to know each other."

"Stop talking," yelled Gary.

"Gary's the intense one," added Rem.

"I can see that." Daniels entered the kitchen and set the plate on the counter. "Anyone want a cinnamon popper? They're delicious."

"I do," said Simon.

"Me, too," said Rem.

"Everybody shut up," yelled Gary. "Both of you sit down. On the far side of the table."

Daniels grabbed the plate. "Fine. Then I'll take the plate with me."

"Bring that coffee, too. I desperately need it." Rem was almost salivating.

"You got it." Daniels walked to the end of the table and sat. Rem took the seat next to him and reached for the coffee. Daniels gave it to him, pulled the covering off the plate and slid it to the center of the table. "Help yourself." He set the bag beside the plate.

Simon's eyes widened, and he moved closer and took a popper.

"Si, get your ass back over here," said Gary, now looking more uncertain than he had before.

Simon ate a popper, closed his eyes, and moaned. "He's right. They're good."

Rem moaned when he sipped his coffee. "That's delicious."

Nibbling his lip, Gary returned to the living room. He was still close enough to fire his gun, but not close enough to tackle. "Come here, Simon."

Simon grabbed another popper and went to join his brother.

Daniels spoke quietly. "What exactly are we dealing with here?"

Rem told Daniels about his morning and how Daniels had arrived just in time to save Rem's butt, assuming Gary would have actually pulled the trigger.

"So these are the two that have been burglarizing homes?" asked Daniels.

"The one and the same."

"But they're so young."

"Tell me about it. But they're getting help from someone named Egg. He's our true ringleader. He's been steering both Gary and Simon down the wrong path."

Daniels watched the brothers talk. "They seem to be doing a good job of that all on their own." He set his forearms on the table. "In case you haven't noticed, they're holding us hostage and they've threatened to kill you."

Rem reached for a popper. "I know it looks bad, but they're dealing with a lot."

Daniels narrowed his eyes. "You seem very sympathetic for someone who could have been shot."

"I don't think he would have shot me." He popped the food into his mouth.

"Sorry to disagree, but you have no idea what he might have done or could still do." He gestured toward the brothers. "They could be planning where to dump our bodies right now."

Rem chewed and swallowed. "Not going to happen. We're too heavy for them to lift."

Daniels smirked. "I think you're missing the point."

"I get what you're saying but they've had a tough year. Their cousin was murdered six months ago. He and Gary were best friends, and Gary blames himself. Plus, they have a mother who doesn't buy them Christmas or birthday gifts. What kind of mom does that?"

Daniels gripped his temples and sighed. "Who's the cousin?"

"You remember Georgios and Titus' unsolved case of a murdered teenager? The victim's name is Trey McDermott. He and Gary were the same age. Seventeen. Simon is fifteen."

Daniels raised a brow. "You have gotten to know them."

"I told you. I've been trying to get past Gary's defenses. Simon's on our side but he's worried about his brother. Apparently, Gary's trying to impress Egg and Egg and his cohorts want us out of the picture."

"So all of this comes down to whether or not Gary decides to go to the dark side?"

"Pretty much. And you just made a *Star Wars* reference. Good for you."

"I've been hanging around you for too long."

"Good to know I'm finally making an impression."

Daniels made a face. "Since day one." He tapped on the table. "So, how do you want to handle this?"

Rem sipped more coffee. "Right now, just keep talking. I think I'm wearing Gary down."

"You just said he might have killed you."

"He's had multiple opportunities, but he hasn't done it. He's just a kid who's terrified and he's trying to work his way through grief just like me. And his little brother is trying to protect him." Rem sat up. "I know a little something about taking the wrong turn at the wrong time. They both just need a little guidance."

"Rem, you're not their therapist. Don't let your empathy for them cloud your judgement. You and I both know that seventeen-year-olds are quite capable of murder."

Rem understood his partner's concern. "Just trust me, okay?" He glanced toward the brothers. "I've got them right where I want them."

"I'll trust you but at some point, we do what we have to do to survive, and Gary's going to have to atone for his actions."

"I get that, but I'd like to try to help them out. Both of them need a break."

Daniels frowned. "Rem, I admire you for that. You obviously feel a connection because of what's happened to you. But that doesn't mean Gary can see things the way you do."

Rem thought of his conversation with Jennie earlier. "What are the odds that these two kids rob my cousin's house on Christmas Eve, when I'm here? I think there's a reason. I'm supposed to help them."

"Well, if that's the case, why am I here?"

Rem considered that. "Back up. In case I'm wrong."

Daniels fell back in his seat. "Great."

Gary's voice rose and then Simon's in an apparent argument. Simon shook his head and Gary told him it wasn't up to him.

"Does that sound good to you?" asked Daniels.

"Not really," said Rem. "I suspect Gary is freaking out about how to deal with two cops now instead of one."

"Let's hope if he had qualms over killing you then that goes for me, too."

"Nobody's killing anybody."

Simon called Gary a jerk and then walked away. Gary scowled at Rem and Daniels, pulled out his phone and made another phone call. "Stick close to me, Twerp. Stop talking to them."

Simon ignored him and grabbed another popper. He sat at the opposite end of the table and ate quietly.

"How's it going over there?" asked Rem.

"Not good," said Simon. "He's convinced we can't leave you two alive. I keep telling him we should just lock you in a room and leave."

Daniels shot a look at Rem. "Yeah. Gary seems like a solid and safe seventeen-year-old kid."

"He's still trying to reach Egg," said Simon.

Rem set his coffee down. "Simon, you know Egg is going to tell Gary the same thing as Buzzard."

"Who's Buzzard?" asked Daniels.

"Egg's buddy," said Rem.

"Oh, that's comforting," said Daniels with an eye roll.

Simon ate the rest of his popper. "I know what Egg will tell him," he said. "I'm trying to get through to Gary, but he won't listen." He licked his fingers and looked at the illuminated Christmas tree on the counter. "Were you telling the truth about the light?"

Rem nodded. "I was."

"What light?" asked Daniels.

Rem pointed toward the yard. "I slept in the shed out back last night, and I had that tree with me." He waved toward the counter. "And Jennie communicated by blinking the light on the top of it." He picked up his drink and sipped it.

Daniels stared at Rem with a blank expression. "Are we in some sort of crazy movie? Is this a practical joke?" He gazed around the room. "Are there cameras on me?"

"I know how it sounds, but it's the truth. Scout's honor." Rem raised two fingers.

"It's three fingers."

"I like two." Rem did his best to explain. "I wasn't drunk, and it wasn't a dream. I swear to you. That light blinked when I asked questions. And I suggested that Gary try it, too. Maybe Trey's around and wants to communicate."

Daniels' mouth hung open.

"Think about it," said Rem. "What better way to get through to Gary than to have his best friend talk to him from the other side?"

"That's your plan?" asked Daniels.

"Yes," said Rem.

"Oh, my God." Daniels rubbed his face. "We're going to die."

"No, we're not," said Rem but he couldn't deny he had a few doubts himself. "At least, I hope not."

Daniels groaned. "Please tell me you have a Plan B."

"Not really."

"Oh, man." Daniels crossed his arms and eyed Simon. "Where are you in all of this?"

"I want to get out of here and go home," said Simon. "Without killing any-one."

"You realize it's not that simple?" asked Daniels.

Somber, Simon nodded. "I know. You've seen us and you know our names. Eventually, you'd find and arrest us."

"Probably," said Daniels.

"That's what scares Gary," said Simon.

"More than murder?" asked Rem. "That makes no sense."

"I told you," said Simon. "He's messed up. Thinks Egg's his ticket to the future, no matter what I say."

"Egg's his ticket to prison," said Daniels.

"We all seem to realize that except Gary," said Rem.

Daniels leaned forward. "Then we need to plan for that. Assuming Trey doesn't come through for us," he offered a flat stare at Rem who shrugged, "then we have to prepare for the worst." He lowered his voice. "Can you help us, Simon?"

Simon looked between the two of them. "I can't betray my brother."

Daniels interlaced his fingers. "Even if it means keeping him out of prison?"

Simon's face fell. "He still might surrender."

"And if he does, great," said Rem. "But if he doesn't..."

Simon took a moment and spoke softly. "What would I have to do?"

Rem watched Gary pace in the living area and speak on the phone. He acted agitated and annoyed.

Daniels kept his voice down. "We need to get closer to him. If we can do that, we might be able to get his gun from him before he does any harm."

Simon swallowed. "Are you going to hurt him?"

"Not if we don't have to," said Rem.

Simon glanced back at his brother, who spoke again into the phone and hung up. He looked over at the table, his eyes haggard and worn. "Come here, Squirt." He shot a glare at Rem and Daniels. "You two stay put."

"I figured," said Rem. He sipped his coffee and made eye contact with Simon, who stood and walked over to Gary. They spoke quietly and Simon's eyes widened. "No way."

"You don't have to stay," said Gary. "You can leave."

"No. I won't."

Gary yelled. "That's the way they want it. You need to get out of here."

Rem tensed and Daniels straightened. "Still want to rely on that light?" asked Daniels.

Rem had to admit the light seemed like an unlikely solution. "What's going on, Gary?" he asked. "What did Egg or Buzzard or whoever you were talking to, say?"

Gary raised his weapon. "You two get up."

Rem's heart rate picked up again and he suspected Daniels' heart was pounding, too. Rem stood.

"Actually, before we do that," said Daniels. "Can I give him his Christmas gift?" He nodded toward Rem. "If we're going to die, it would be a nice parting gesture."

"You brought me my gift?" asked Rem. "I thought we were doing gifts tonight."

"We are, or at least we were," said Daniels. "But I wanted to give this to you early."

"Oh, how nice." Rem spoke to Gary. "You mind?"

"You're stalling," said Gary.

"Can you blame us?" asked Rem.

Gary hesitated. "You were lying to me earlier, weren't you?" he asked Rem.

Rem put his coffee back on the table. "About what?"

Gary glowered and spoke to Daniels. "Your partner told me something bad happened to him this year. What was it?"

Daniels paused. "His girlfriend, Jennie, who he loved very much, was killed by a drunk driver in a car accident nine months ago." He stilled. "He's grieving, just like you."

Gary held still but his jaw clenched. "Fine. Give him his gift. Si, you stay with me."

Daniels had set the bag on the table. "Thank you." He reached for it, slid it closer and pulled out a wrapped slender package. He handed it to Rem. "Merry Christmas, Buddy."

Rem took it, wondering what Daniels was planning. "It better not be a book."

"God forbid you should read."

Rem ripped open the wrapping and pulled out a smooth wooden board with a slim border. Words were etched into it. He read it and his throat tightened. It was a plaque just like his mother had given him all those years ago during their hamburger Christmas. Not believing his eyes, he reread it.

Trust me, buddy. It's going to get better. I promise.

Love, your best friend.

A crude hamburger had been carved above the words and on the back was a hook to hang it.

"I figured you needed a new one," said Daniels. "It's not my best hamburger, but you get the gist."

His emotions swelling, and his tears rising, Rem sniffed. "It's perfect. You made this?"

"Been working on it all week." He put a hand on Rem's shoulder. "Do you like it?"

"I love it." He stared at it in disbelief. Seeing it brought back so many memories. "I'm going to hang it in the bathroom, so I see it every morning." He lowered it. "Thank you."

"You bet. I'm glad you like it."

"What is it?" asked Simon from across the room.

Rem noted Simon's and even Gary's curious eyes, and he realized why Daniels had wanted him to open it. "It's uh…"

"It's what?" asked Gary.

Rem took a deep breath and hoped this would work. "It's a message from the dead."

"A what?" asked Gary.

Holding the plaque, Rem took slow steps toward Gary. Daniels stayed behind him. Getting closer, Rem held the plaque out. "I think it's a message for you, too."

Gary hesitated, but then leaned in to read the plaque. Simon read it, too, and he sucked in a breath. "That's something Trey would have said. And it has a hamburger on it like at Showburger's." He pointed. "It even says 'Love, your best friend.'"

"I can read," said Gary, but his agitation had lessened, and he studied the plaque. "That's not for me, though."

"Isn't it?" asked Rem. "The people we love find ways to communicate. What are the odds I'd open this in front of you on Christmas Day? This is a message for you just as much as it is for me. Maybe the tree didn't blink, but this is definitely a sign." He paused. "Trey's talking to you...but are you listening?"

Gary stepped back, the gun still raised, but his anger had diminished. "You're just screwing with me."

"No, we're not," said Rem. "We want to help you. So does Trey. I think he has a lot to do with why I'm here. It's not an accident." Now that they were nearer to Gary, Rem was tempted to reach out but didn't want to spook him. "You can trust us."

"Listen to him," said Simon.

Gary shook his head. "Egg's my friend now. Not Trey."

"Why do you think Egg can help you?" asked Daniels. "And not us?"

"Because you're cops. Egg says I can't trust cops. They lie."

"Some cops might lie, but not us." Rem stepped closer and Gary didn't move. "I'm not saying it's going to be easy, but with a little hard work, you can get your life back. You can't get that with Egg."

"Guys like Egg eat kids like you for lunch," said Daniels. "That's why they recruit teenagers who are in lousy situations. They're looking for a group to belong to. A family. Egg provides that, but only for so long. Once he doesn't need you anymore, he'll discard you and move on to the next kid."

Gary's anger flared. "I'm not a kid."

"No," said Rem. "You're not. You're seventeen and when you turn eighteen, you're going to have some hard decisions to make before you end up somewhere you can't come back from." He nodded at Daniels. "He and I have seen teenagers like you do terrible things and they either end up in prison, dead, or wishing they were dead. I don't want that to happen to you. And neither does your brother."

A trickle of sweat ran down Gary's temple. "I can take care of my brother."

"Not by handing him over to Egg, you can't," said Daniels. "Egg will eat him up, too."

"Just give me the gun, Gary," said Rem. "Aren't you tired of all the worry and fear? Robbing houses will only lead to bigger crimes and bigger penalties. Maybe it's time to stop running now instead of later."

Gary's hand trembled. "I don't know."

"What do you think Trey's saying to you right now?" asked Daniels.

Gary didn't say a word.

Simon gasped. "Gary," he pointed. "Look at the tree."

Rem turned along with Daniels. The light at the top of the tree was blinking. Rem felt the familiar warmth in his gut return. "Looks like Trey agrees."

The light stopped blinking and Gary stared at it, his eyes glittering with unshed tears. "Trey. Is that you?"

The light blinked again.

Rem smiled, and Simon stood in shock. Daniels stared at the light in surprise, too.

"I'd say that's a yes," said Rem. He spoke to Daniels. "Told ya I talked to Jennie."

Daniels eyed the light again. "I stand corrected."

Rem looked back at Gary. "What do you say? You ready to start fresh?"

Gary sniffed and a tear escaped and trickled down his cheek. "I hate robbing houses."

"It's a lousy way to make a living," said Daniels.

Gary stood quietly but then his arm relaxed and Rem blew out a sigh of relief when Gary lowered the gun. "You're a brave kid...sorry...man." He reached for the gun when the back door slammed open.

Everyone jumped, Gary stiffened and raised the gun again, and Rem and Daniels swiveled to face the door. A man, tall and thin, wearing fancy clothes and sparkly jewelry, stood in the kitchen, holding a large gun which he aimed at Daniels and Rem. He grinned and a gold tooth sparkled in the light.

"Egg," said Gary in surprise. "What are you doing here?"

"Well, well, well," said Egg, eyeing everyone in the room until he settled his gaze on Rem and Daniels. "Who do we have here?"

Chapter Ten

DANIELS DIDN'T MOVE AND neither did anyone else, but he knew their situation had just gone from bad to much worse. He glanced at Rem and knew his partner was thinking the same thing.

Egg kicked the door shut but kept his gun trained on Daniels and Rem. His hand didn't shake, and Daniels sensed that Egg would have no problem using it.

"What's up, G?" said Egg, his stare never wavering. "Hey, Si." Neither boy answered. "Looks like you two are having an interesting Christmas."

Gary, aiming his gun at Rem, stammered. "Wh...what are you doing here?"

"I heard about your little fiasco. My damn phone kept ringing, and I finally talked to Buzzard. He told me about your problem. I'd have sent him but he's in LA for the damn holiday."

"You didn't have to come," said Gary. "Buzzard told me what to do."

"Let's just say my confidence that you would follow through was lacking." Egg cursed. "When you two screw it up, you do it big, don't you?"

"I can handle it," said Gary. His apprehension gone, he blinked back any unshed tears.

"You're taking your damn sweet time." Egg stood rigid in the room. "I know how it is. The first time can be hard, so I'd thought I'd help you out. You're going to owe me for screwing up my Christmas, though."

"You told us the house would be empty, but it wasn't," argued Gary. "He was here." He jabbed his gun at Rem.

"Sorry to spoil the fun," said Rem.

Egg, his focus never leaving Daniels or Rem, twisted his lips into an ugly smirk. "If you're going to work for me, G, you better learn how to handle the unexpected. It comes with the territory. If you can't do that, then you're worthless to me."

Gary straightened. "I said I can handle it."

"This should have been over with and you out of here with the goods." He flicked his gaze at Gary. "You goin' soft on me?"

Gary shook his head. "No. I'm not."

"Good. Glad to hear it," said Egg. He narrowed his eyes at Daniels. "Now let's take care of business and get back to Christmas."

Daniels determined that they were out of time. Whatever Egg's plan was, he wasn't going to hesitate like Gary. He deduced that Rem was close enough to handle Gary, but he was straight in the line of Egg's fire. The timing would have to be perfect, or he'd be shot dead. "You realize we're cops?" he said. "You shoot us and the whole force will come down on you."

Egg didn't seem concerned. "I didn't get to where I am by being stupid." He snickered. "We'll kill both you assholes and leave your bodies behind. We'll take off and you two won't be discovered until tonight at the earliest. By then, we'll be long gone. We'll lay low for a while, but no one will trace this back to us."

"You drove here, didn't you?" asked Rem. "It's Christmas morning. People are home."

"Cars can be dumped." Egg chuckled. "Assuming anyone bothers to even look. As you say, it's Christmas morning. Kids are opening their gifts. Mom and Dad are tired. In this neighborhood, nobody's paying any attention."

Simon, who'd been standing quietly to the side, his eyes round as dinner plates, spoke softly. "We can't do this."

"Shut up, Simon," said Egg. "Your brother and I will take care of this. Just keep your mouth shut."

Simon eyed Gary, his face a mask of concern. "Don't do this, Gary. You know it's wrong. Don't listen to him."

His face taut, Gary swallowed. "Are you sure this is the best idea, Egg?"

"You got any better ones?" asked Egg. "You want to free them so they can find and arrest you? And then threaten you with jail time in order to get to me? And when you hand me over, they put you in jail anyway?" He scoffed. "No way. You can't trust cops. I told you that."

"Don't listen to him, Gary," said Rem, still holding the plaque. "You want to know what will happen?" He slowly set the plaque down on a small table beside the couch. "You kill us and then Egg kills you, because he won't trust you to keep your mouth shut. He'll kill Simon, too."

Egg shot a nasty look at Rem. "He's lying to get you to back off. I don't kill my crew."

"Unless they become liabilities," said Daniels, not taking his eyes off Egg. The moment he had an opportunity, he would have to act. "Right, Egg?"

Egg's grip tightened on his gun and Daniels held his breath. "I shoot this one, G. You shoot the other. You got it?"

Gary's expression faltered.

"You can't kill them," said Simon. He approached Egg. "Please. Gary's not like you."

Egg pulled back his free hand and smacked Simon across the face, but his aim on Daniels never faltered. "You're such a pain-in-the-ass. I never should have taken you on. I only did it because of your brother. I should have trusted my instincts."

Simon fell back and grabbed his cheek.

"Simon," said Rem, his eyes darting between Gary and Egg. "Stay back, okay? Just go to the corner."

Daniels hoped Simon would listen and get out of the line of fire.

"Do as he says, Squirt." Gary narrowed his eyes at Egg. "You shouldn't have hit him."

Simon rubbed his red cheek. Blinking back tears, he stepped back. "Gary, please don't."

"It's okay, Si," said Gary. "I can take care of myself."

Egg chuckled. "Isn't that sweet? It's about time you became a man, G. I'm glad I'll be here to see it. You ready?"

Daniels braced and took a small step closer to Egg. He could see Rem do the same with Gary.

Gary frowned at Egg. "Simon's right. This is a bad idea. We can't kill cops."

Daniels felt a small sense of relief but knew they weren't out of the woods. "Smart move, Gary."

"You're more of a man now than ever," said Rem.

Egg's face twisted more than before. "You stupid shit. You're going to listen to them instead of me? Just who the hell do you think you're dealing with?"

Gary raised his voice. "I just think—"

"Nobody asked you to think," yelled Egg. "You either do this or I shoot everyone, including you. And I'll start with your dipshit brother."

Gary set his jaw. "Egg. Listen. This isn't smart."

"You think you know better than me?" asked Egg. "You think you can tell me what to do?" He sneered. "You and your brother are as stupid as your cousin. I put him in his place, and I'll put you in yours."

Gary froze but his face furrowed. "What did you say?"

Simon stared at Egg in disbelief.

"I should have known to stay the hell away from you two," said Egg. "Nothing but trouble. You're a waste of space. I strung you along because I felt sorry for you, but not anymore." He spat at them. "I should have told Buzzard to take care of you the way he took care of Trey."

Daniels clenched his fingers. Egg had ordered Trey's murder. He watched as Gary's face morphed from uncertainty to rage.

"You killed Trey?" asked Gary, his voice low.

"I did what had to be done. Kid got in my face and paid the price," said Egg. "Just like you will."

"Gary," said Rem, holding up a hand. "Listen to me…"

"Shut up, cop," yelled Egg. "Last chance, G. Are you going to man up, or die?"

Gary made a strangled sound, moved the gun from Rem and pointed it at Egg. "How could you kill him?"

Daniels' heart rate doubled its pace. He and Rem were about to find them-selves in the middle of a shootout.

Egg chuckled but didn't sound amused. "Put that damn gun down."

"No. I won't," said Gary.

Daniels made brief eye contact with Rem. They were going to have to do something, and fast.

"That's a death sentence, kid," said Egg.

"Not if I kill you first," said Gary, his eyes filling with tears. "You killed Trey. How could you do that?"

"He got in my business. A message needed to be sent." Egg kept his gun aimed at Daniels. "That's the way it works, you shithead. Now take that damn gun off me or I'll take your brother next."

Gary exploded. "You son-of-a-bitch."

"Gary, no," said Simon.

In the second of silence that followed, Egg's eyes narrowed to slits, Rem kept his eyes on Gary, and Daniels prepared when music suddenly blared.

Egg jumped and Daniels launched himself.

Hearing the music, Rem saw Daniels react and Rem shot forward and grabbed Gary's gun. He got a hold of it before Gary could fire and pushed it away from Egg, Daniels, and Simon.

"No," yelled Gary.

Rem wrenched the gun from Gary's hand and got his arm around him.

"Let me shoot him," screamed Gary, who struggled against Rem.

Rem took the gun and held Gary back. He didn't need him attacking Egg and getting caught up in the scuffle with Daniels.

Daniels had grabbed for Egg's gun and gripped it and Egg's wrist while Egg fought back, but Daniels was way bigger and stronger, and he shoved Egg against the wall. Egg grunted. The gun went off and fired into the ceiling.

Rem dropped to the ground and pulled Gary down with him. Simon ran over and Rem yanked him down, too, and dragged him next to Gary.

Egg screamed and cursed but Daniels held him against the wall, reared a knee back and brought it straight up into Egg's groin.

Egg made a grunt, his face went flat and white and he dropped like a rock. Daniels pulled the gun away as Egg slid to the floor in front of him. Daniels slid the gun into his waistband and quickly searched Egg for any other weapons. Not finding one, he studied Egg's inert form. "Merry Christmas...asshole." Breathless, he looked back at Rem, who hovered over Gary and Simon. "You okay?"

Rem nodded. "Doing great."

"You got any cuffs?"

"Nope."

Daniels looked around. "Okay." He walked to a nearby lamp, pulled the cord from the wall, and brought the lamp over to Egg, who was no longer frozen in shock and was now writhing on the floor. Daniels flipped him over, pulled his arms back, and wrapped the cord several times around Egg's wrists. He set the lamp on the back of Egg's legs. "That ought to hold you." He pulled out his phone. "I'll call it in."

Seeing the situation under control, Rem sat up. He set Gary's gun down, away from Gary's reach. Simon looked up, too.

"You all right?" asked Rem.

Simon nodded.

Gary hadn't moved.

"Gary?" asked Rem. "How are you?"

Gary kept his head down. "He killed Trey."

Simon put his hand on his brother's back. "It's okay."

"I didn't know," said Gary. His voice shook and he gripped the floor.

Rem understood his agony. "You're going to get through this, Gary."

"How could I not know?" His breath caught. "I never should have..." He held his hand over his mouth.

"You were just doing the best you could," said Rem. "Just take it easy. It's all over now." He put his hand on Gary's arm.

"I...I...just..." A sob bubbled up. "Why did he have to go? I miss him so much."

Hearing Gary's anguish and relating to it, Rem's chest tightened. "I know you do, kid. I know."

Gary's sobs came harder and faster and he tried to talk but all Rem could make out was, "I hate my life."

Simon wrapped himself around his brother, his own tears threatening.

His face red and his cheeks wet, Gary wiped at his face. "I'm sorry, Simon. I'm so, so sorry." He could barely get the words out.

Fighting back his own tears, Rem pulled Gary closer, and the teenager's face fell into his shoulder. His sobs intensified and his tears soaked Rem's shirt. Doing his best to hold it together, Rem put an arm around him and let him weep.

Chapter Eleven

HOLDING HIS GIFTS, REM knocked on Daniels' door. Marjorie opened it. Her blonde hair brushed her shoulders, and she wore a white t-shirt with Santa on it and blue jeans. She smiled. "Hey, Rem. Come on in."

"Thanks." He entered and walked into the kitchen. "Merry Christmas."

"Merry Christmas, although after your morning, it almost wasn't. Thank God you and Gordon are okay." She took his gifts. "I'll put these on the table."

"It was definitely touch and go."

She set the gifts down next to two others on the dining table and returned to the kitchen. "Gordon told me about those two teenagers. I can't believe it. So much for a quiet Christmas."

"It all worked out in the end."

"How are the two boys? Gordon said you were going to help them out?"

Rem nodded. After the police had arrived, he'd spent the rest of his day walking Gary and Simon through the whole process of being booked into juvenile detention, telling them to stay positive and they'd be okay. He'd met their mother, who was contrite and felt terrible about leaving them, but Rem didn't have much sympathy for her. After doing some digging, he'd learned the boys had a grandfather in San Francisco that the mom had not spoken to in over two years. Rem had persuaded her to call him and that there was no shame in asking for help. The grandfather had agreed to travel there the next day to do what he could to assist his daughter and grandsons.

Since it was Christmas, Gary and Simon would have to stay the night in juvenile detention, but at least they were together and would get a square meal, a place to sleep and people to watch out for them. It wasn't ideal but Rem wondered if that would be an improvement over going home. Rem had promised he'd check in on them the next day. "I'm going to try my best. They're two of the rare few who might make it through this and still have a chance at a decent life."

"Well, if you're going to be there for them, then they have a great shot."

"I appreciate that. I hope you're right." He looked around. "Where's Daniels?"

She grabbed a chip from a bowl on the counter. "He's out back, grilling our dinner."

Rem took a chip, too. "He's grilling, huh? What's on the menu?" He could almost hear the steaks sizzling.

"He told me to tell you it was a surprise. He should be in soon." She popped the chip in her mouth and ate it. "You want a beer?"

"I'd love one."

She opened the fridge and pulled out two beers. She gave one to Rem and held the other one. "I'll tell him you're here."

Rem twisted the cap off of his bottle. "Thanks."

Marjorie went outside and a few seconds later, she and Daniels returned. "Hey," he said, holding his beer. "How was the rest of your day? How'd it go with Simon and Gary?"

Rem gave him an update. "I think with Egg in custody and Gary and Simon willing to testify against him and Buzzard, they'll get some leeway."

"I'm sure they will. Plus, we'll put in a good word for them."

"Lozano talked to L.A. about Buzzard. Apparently, it's not his first brush with the law and they knew who we were talking about. Buzzard's Christmas, and freedom, ended about an hour ago."

"Not surprising. Let's hope he and Egg stay behind bars for a long time."

Rem agreed. "That would be a nice gift from Santa. Just get a good sleep tonight because with everything that happened today, we've got a busy day tomorrow."

"I suspected as much."

"I talked to Chico, too. After what happened, he's cutting his trip short and coming home."

"That's too bad, but not surprising. I suppose it could be a lot worse though."

"Definitely." Rem sipped his beer. "What's so secretive about dinner? You making something illegal?"

"Nothing that exciting. It should be done in a second." He put an arm around Marjorie, who was washing a dish in the sink. "You want some wine, hon?"

Marjorie smiled back at him. "I beat you to it. It's already open on the table."

Daniels glanced toward the dining area. Rem did, too. It was already set with the gifts to one side and an uncorked bottle of wine beside them. Rem couldn't help but think back to last year, but determined not to be sad, he shook the memories off. Thinking of his talk with Jennie that morning, he felt better knowing she was near.

"As usual, you're on top of it." Daniels held his beer out to Rem. "Here. Take this, I'll get the food."

Rem took his bottle.

"Have a seat," said Marjorie, heading toward the table.

Rem followed, pulled out a chair and sat. He set the beers down, and Marjorie grabbed the chips and placed them beside the bottle of wine. Rem wondered why there were chips for Christmas dinner. It seemed odd but figured it wasn't his meal, so he shrugged it off.

A few seconds later, Daniels returned, holding a platter with hamburger patties and buns. He set them on the kitchen counter and, seeing the burgers, Rem chuckled.

Daniels opened the fridge and pulled out a plate filled with sliced tomatoes, lettuce, and pickles, and he grabbed mayo and mustard.

"You made hamburgers," said Rem.

Daniels shut the fridge and set the plate with the condiments next to the platter. "I sure did."

"I thought it was strange for a Christmas dinner, but he said you would understand," said Marjorie.

"I do," said Rem, recalling his dinner by the pool with his mother years earlier. "Nothing like a hamburger for Christmas." He stood and eyed the platter.

"And I added extra cheese to yours," said Daniels. He pointed to a burger that was covered in cheddar.

"I picked well when they were doling out partners." Rem picked up his plate.

"That you did," said Daniels. "Dig in."

They helped themselves to the burgers and chips and enjoyed their meal. Rem reflected a few times and thought of Jennie, but the laughter and conversation between them made it easier. Once the meal was done, he shoved his gifts toward Daniels. "Time for the good stuff." He slid one to Marjorie, too.

"You didn't have to get me a gift," she said with a smile.

"Of course, I did. You put up with him." He gestured toward Daniels. "That deserves something."

"You've got a point," she said. She patted Daniels hand. "You first."

"Okay," said Daniels. He ripped open his first gift and chuckled when he saw it was a Chia Pet in the shape of a dog. He held it up. "You got me one."

"I wanted to get you the herb garden starter kit, but somebody else got first dibs."

Daniels smirked. "That's what you get for shopping at the last minute."

"An herb garden would be fantastic," said Marjorie. "I've always wanted one of those."

"At least I found that," said Rem, pointing. "I figure everyone should have a Chia Pet at some point in their lives."

"That's great," said Daniels. "Dad wouldn't approve, though."

"Then we'll keep it between us."

"Open the other one," said Marjorie.

Daniels set the Chia Pet aside and opened the other package. He pulled it out and stilled. It was a picture of the four of them from the previous Christmas standing around the tree in Rem's apartment. They were all smiling and holding their drinks. Rem had enlarged it and placed it in a nice frame. Just seeing it made Rem's throat tighten. "I decided it was time for you to have a Christmas picture."

Daniels stared at the photo. "It's beautiful." His eyes watered. "I love it." He showed it to Marjorie.

Taking a breath, Rem kept his emotions in check. It was hard to look at the picture, but he was grateful it had been taken. It was a memory he didn't want to lose.

"Rem, that's perfect." Marjorie was a little teary-eyed herself. "You should hang it in the front entry, honey. Or maybe put it on the shelf by the stairwell."

"I will." Daniels took the picture back. "Thanks, Rem."

"You're welcome." Rem sniffed and spoke to Marjorie. "Your turn." He was glad he could move onto the next gift before his fragile emotional hold broke.

Marjorie wiped at a tear and smiled. "Okay." She pulled off the wrapping and laughed. "It's the herb garden starter kit." She held it up.

Daniels grinned. "Nice choice," he said to Rem.

Rem gestured toward the gift. "I figured you two could share and I suspect she'd take better care of it than you."

"I know she would," said Daniels.

"I will," said Marjorie. "I can't wait to use it. Thank you."

"You're welcome," said Rem.

Daniels set his gifts aside and grabbed one of the two left on the table. "This one's from Chico. He asked me to give it to you."

Rem took it. "Let's see what Chico came up with." He opened it and pulled out darts and a dart board. He smiled. "Figures. We went and got a beer not long ago and played darts. He kicked my butt. I guess this is his way to get me to practice."

"You are pretty awful at darts," said Daniels.

"You aren't much better," replied Rem. He set the dart board aside.

"We'll practice together." Daniels grabbed the last gift. "There's one more." It was a small box and he slid it toward Rem.

"Is this from you?" asked Rem. "But you already got me the plaque."

"This is from me and Marjorie."

"I hope you like it," said Marjorie.

Rem took the gift. "I'm sure I will." He removed the wrapping and opened the box. Inside was a ticket. He picked it up.

"It's a ticket to that reggae band you and Jennie liked," said Daniels. "They're playing at the Pavilion on New Year's Eve." The Pavilion was a restaurant and music venue where you could eat, dance, and enjoy live music. "The three of us have reservations at eight o'clock. We can have dinner and either stay there and ring in the new year or come back here and do it together in peace and quiet, or you can go home and ring it in by yourself. It will be completely up to you."

Rem eyed the ticket. He'd had no idea what he was going to do on New Year's Eve, but this seemed like the perfect solution. "That's a great idea."

"Are you sure?" asked Marjorie. "We didn't want you to be alone, but we didn't want to intrude either. If you'd rather not go, that's fine."

Rem sighed but smiled. "I'm being honest. I appreciate this." He fiddled with the ticket. "I was dreading New Year's, but this will help. I'd be happy to spend it with you."

Daniels sat up. "I was hoping you'd say yes."

"Thank you both." He put the ticket back in the box, grateful he no longer had to worry about the next holiday. "That means a lot."

"You're welcome," said Marjorie. Her phone rang and she pulled it out of her pocket. "It's Granddad. I'll take it in the other room. Be right back." She answered. "Granddad? Hey. Merry Christmas." She walked out of the kitchen.

"You doing okay?" asked Daniels. "Especially after our harrowing morning?"

Rem set his napkin on the table. "I'm hanging in there. I'm just glad it worked out with Gary and Simon. I was beginning to think my grand plan had failed."

"If it hadn't been for that tree, it might have."

Rem picked up his beer. "I don't know if it was Jennie or Trey who turned on that music, but we owe them our lives." He took a drink.

"Thank God for messages from the dead."

Rem set his bottle down. "I took the tree home, by the way. Chico's going to have to fight me for it."

"I don't blame you." He paused. "You really think either Jennie or Trey turned on that music?"

"Don't you?"

Daniels rested an arm on the table. "I tend to be skeptical, but I'd like to think so."

"Me, too, and unless I discover a short in the tree, then I'll choose to believe they were looking out for us."

Daniels picked up his framed photo. "Thanks again for this. It's really special."

Rem looked at their smiling faces in the picture. "I made one for myself, too. It's hard to look at but also good for me." He paused. "And that plaque you made me is hanging in my bathroom. That's good for me, too."

"That's what I was hoping." Daniels set the picture down. "Because your mom was right back then and still is. It will get better."

"I can only hope." Rem picked at his napkin. "After what happened today with Gary and Simon, I've been doing a lot of reflecting." He took a second to gather himself. "I wanted to thank you for everything. This year has been…well…unbearable." He cleared his throat. "And I wouldn't have survived it without your help."

Daniels leaned in. "It's what partners do. I was happy to be there for you."

Rem shook his head. "It couldn't have been easy. You and Jennie were friends. You were grieving, too."

"We were all struggling, and we all helped each other, whether you realize it or not. You processing your grief helped me process mine, and Marjorie's."

Rem sighed. "I don't know about that. I've just been trying to put one foot in front of the other."

"You're getting there but be patient with yourself. Next year will be better."

"It has to be. I can't handle much more."

Daniels picked up his Chia Pet. "You've been through some tough times, Rem, and you've survived. I think you're stronger than you realize."

Rem eyed Daniels' gift. "At least I never got denied a Chia Pet growing up."

Daniels raised the side of his lip. "That was pure torture."

"I bet." He thought of that morning in the shed. "You know, when I was talking to Jennie through that light this morning, she inferred that it was her time to go, and that I might uh,...or could, fall in love again."

"Is that so hard to believe?"

"It is, yes. But I wish I knew why she had to go." He took a deep breath. "Why did she leave me?"

Daniels set the Chia Pet aside. "I wish I knew the answer. Maybe she knows something you don't."

"Like what?"

"Maybe she left because she can do more for you on the other side. Think about what happened today."

"Despite that, I'd rather have her on this side."

"I know." Daniels quieted. "But maybe it's time to trust that she knows what she's doing, and she loved you enough to leave you. Who knows what's in store for you next, Rem? Maybe that's her evil plan. To watch out for you."

Rem sniffed and dabbed at an unshed tear. "I don't know if I will ever have the courage to love again."

"Something tells me Jennie has other ideas." He set his napkin in his plate. "And when the time is right, you'll know it." He interlaced his fingers. "You just have to have a little faith."

Rem swallowed and blinked back tears. "One day at a time, right?"

"And I'll be with you every step of the way, just like Jennie."

"I know you will. Just keep supplying chocolate and tacos. That will help."

"You got it." Daniels picked up his beer. "Here's to a new year and new memories. May there be many." He raised his bottle.

Rem sniffed again and raised his own. "Hear. Hear."

"Happy hamburger Christmas, partner."

Sad but deeply thankful for his many blessings, Rem clinked his bottle against Daniels' and smiled softly. "Happy hamburger Christmas, partner."

∞∞∞∞

Want more from J. T. Bishop? Sign up for her newsletter at jtbishopautho r.com. Get the Daniels and Remalla prequel novella, *The Girl and the Gunshot*, available to subscribers only, for free, in addition to extra content, plus opportunities for more free books.

I hope you enjoyed *A Hamburger Christmas*. If you enjoyed Daniels and Remalla, then you're in luck, because they have a couple of series for you to enjoy. They'll battle crime and supernatural forces that will challenge their beliefs and fortitude. (I have a penchant for mystery thrillers with a paranormal edge.)

First up is the *Family or Foe Saga*. This is a four-book series where Daniels and Remalla are introduced. A killer with powerful abilities is out for revenge against those he believes wronged him. Can Daniels and Remalla catch him before he exacts his will and kills them, too?

Enjoy an excerpt of *First Cut*, book one in the saga, below.

Next up is Detectives Daniels' and Remalla's own series. They'll battle dangerous enemies with harbored grudges, unique abilities, cruel intentions, and psychopathic tendencies. Through it all, they'll have to rely on each other to survive.

Either of these series can be read first, but if you like to read in order, start with *Family or Foe*.

And if you enjoy Daniels and Remalla, then you'll want to meet the Redstones. Former Texas Ranger and medium Mason Redstone and his sister Mikey, introduced in *Of Breath and Blood* (book two in the Daniels and Remalla series), run a paranormal investigation firm where they'll take the cases others won't and risk their lives in the process. This series is a crossover with Daniels and Remalla.

Note: Because the Daniels and Remalla books and The Redstone Chronicles are a spinoff and crossover series, they share an overarching story, and the characters from each are mentioned or appear in all the books, so reading both is ideal. The books published alternate between both series. A list of books in chronological order follows below.

Or, if you like light sci-fi with urban fantasy and a delicious romance thrown in, then check out Bishop's first series, *The Red-Line Trilogy*. One woman holds the key to unlocking an antique mirror that contains secrets crucial to the survival of a mysterious community. One man, assigned to protect her, will risk everything to keep her alive, but when he falls for her, will their destiny be enough to save them both?

And the Red-Line series continues with the four-book sister series to the trilogy, *The Fletcher Family Saga*. A distant but deadly threat risks the lives of three unique siblings, but life can't stop because of who they are. They'll endure love, loss and a dangerous enemy determined to destroy them.

Either the trilogy or sister series can be read first. Take your pick. Boxed sets are available, too!

A Note from J.T.

I LOVE TO HEAR from my fans about my books and I hope you enjoyed *A Hamburger Christmas*. I've been wanting to write a Christmas story for a while, and I thought Remalla and Daniels would be the perfect fit for it. I love their friendship and banter, plus there's plenty of backstory to cover.

In the book *First Cut*, where I introduce Rem and Daniels, Jennie had died eighteen months prior. This novella allowed me to explore the effects of her death on Remalla and how he handled her loss, especially at Christmastime.

I also appreciate touching and heartwarming stories and those abound during the holidays. When it comes to gift giving, it's always fun when characters give each other presents with deep meaning. I had to think about what Rem and Daniels would give each other that would elicit the emotion and demonstrate their tight bond. I had an image in my mind of Remalla and his mom sitting around a pool eating hamburgers. I decided they were there because Rem's dad had screwed up again. Then I imagined Rem's mom giving him a special plaque with a special message. Of course, that would allow the perfect opportunity for Daniels to give Rem something similar.

We also get a chance to delve a little into Daniels' backstory with his father, too. Rem's gift to Daniels shows that Daniels wasn't the only one thinking about his partner. The picture of the couples together was a great way to provide a final touching tribute to the past while also helping both men to move forward.

I hope this story made you smile and even sniffle a time or two. I shed some tears while writing it and hope the message of friendship, love, acceptance, saying goodbye and welcoming new beginnings resonated. Here's wishing you your own Hamburger Christmas.

Reviews are a huge plus and big help for an author and potential readers. I would love it if you could please take a couple of minutes to leave a quick review for *A Hamburger Christmas*. And if you'd like, please leave a few comments, too.

As always, thank you for your time and readership. It is deeply valued and appreciated.

Now, on to the next book!

Books in Chronological Order

ALTHOUGH RECOMMENDED BUT NOT required, in case you prefer to read in order...

Lost Dreams
Of Mind and Madness
Lost Chances
Of Power and Pain
Lost Hope
Of Love and Loss
Lost Lives
Dominion
Lost Time
Illusions

Acknowledgements

ANOTHER BOOK IS COMPLETE, and again, I have many to thank. This doesn't happen alone, and I am indebted to family and friends for their help, support and encouragement. It is truly appreciated.

I also want to thank my Beta and ARC teams. You guys keep me on my toes, ensure I write a great story, and help with early reviews. Thank you for being honest and offering your guidance.

I love writing about the bonds between loving family, deep friendships and the ties that hold them together. Plus, my fascination with the unknown thrown into the mix makes for a satisfying story and hopefully, adds a little more thrill for my readers.

I especially want to thank my fans. Hearing from you and knowing that you're enjoying my books makes all the hard work worthwhile. None of this would matter without your tremendous support. If I can help you escape from this crazy world for a short period each day, then I've done my job.

Here's to more stories, more fun, and more time for yourself. If you can have a little of that each day, you're on the right track.

Enjoy an excerpt from First Cut, Book One in The Family or Foe Saga.

SEEING THE GUN, DANIELS pulled his weapon, aiming at the woman. He stood at a diagonal to Remalla, so his partner was not in the line of fire. His heart rate tripled, and he watched Rem hold up his arms.

"Drop the gun!" he yelled.

The woman glanced at him, but she held the gun on Rem. "Who are you? What do you want?"

Rem kept his hands visible. "Take it easy. We're cops," he said. "I'm going to take my badge out." He slowly moved his hand toward his back pocket, making it obvious so the woman could see he wasn't going for his weapon.

The woman, eyes wide with uncertainty, kept looking between Rem and Daniels. "You, too," she said to Daniels.

Daniels didn't move. "Take that gun off my partner."

Rem pulled out his badge and opened it. "I'm Detective Remalla and this is my partner, Detective Daniels. Are you Jill Jacobs? Sergeant Merchant told us where to find you. All we want to do is talk." He kept his hands up and spoke in a soothing voice.

The woman hesitated. "Talk about what?"

"Drop the gun first," yelled Daniels.

Remalla took a small step forward, and Daniels held his breath. "We didn't mean to scare you. We want to talk about the Makeup Artist."

Even from a distance, Daniels could see her face pale. She stared for a second, her forehead furrowed, and then she relaxed her stance, lowered her weapon and tucked it into the waistband of her shorts.

Rem dropped his hands and glanced back at Daniels, who let go of a lungful of held breath and holstered his gun. He debated arresting her, but realized she wasn't a threat and they would need her cooperation. He walked over to his partner but stayed on alert.

"You okay?" asked Daniels to Rem.

Rem took a shaky breath. "That'll wake you up."

"Still scared of zombies?"

Rem didn't answer as the woman approached with wariness.

"Jill Jacobs?" asked Rem.

She walked past them and toward her beach chair. Reaching it, she grabbed another bottle from the bucket. "That's me."

They followed. "You want to tell us why you pull guns on strangers?" asked Daniels.

She twisted the cap off. "You came up behind me," she said, taking a healthy swig.

"It's a public beach," said Rem.

She waved. "Does it look public?"

"You go around waving guns, you're going to get arrested," said Daniels.

"I'll take my chances," she said, and sat in the chair. She removed her weapon and put it beside her, careful to do it slowly to not alarm Rem or Daniels.

"Well, we don't mean to interrupt your 'me' time, but we'd like to ask you a few questions," said Rem.

"Can't promise I'll answer." She took another swig.

Rem raised a brow at Daniels. "You were a cop in Seattle, right? Worked on the Makeup Artist case?"

"That was a long time ago. In another life," she said, resting her head back.

Daniels nodded. "Been in the RV park long?"

She watched the waves. "A while."

"It's a charming place, but a little crazy." Rem paused. "It matches your personality." She gave him a quick appraisal but didn't respond. "Your sergeant thought you'd be helpful to us. We're working on a case you might have some insight on."

She took another pull, and Daniels wondered how often Jill Jacobs drank. It was a lot based on how fast she was draining her beer.

"He wasted your time. I can't help you," she answered.

"You worked on the Makeup Artist case in Seattle, didn't you?" asked Daniels.

She hesitated, picking on the bottle's label. "I did."

"Then I'm pretty sure you can help us," said Rem. "We've—"

"You don't get it," said Jill. "I don't want to help you."

Rem crossed his arms and set his jaw, and Daniels knew his partner was getting agitated. He could be cool and calm with a gun pointed at him but could lose his temper with an uncooperative stranger in a heartbeat.

"Fine," Daniels interjected, before Rem could say something less fruitful. "We'll go back and let our captain know that the two victims who were slaughtered in the last six weeks and their families are no closer to finding justice and the madman who did it. Even though he's already stalking his next victim and will continue to enjoy the same freedoms as you and me. We'll be sure to let your Sergeant Merchant know that his suggestion was a waste of our time."

Her face pinched, and she picked off a chunk of the label. Daniels saw her swallow.

"Merchant gave us your name for a reason," said Rem.

"He did," she said. Daniels could barely hear her over the waves.

"Listen," said Rem. "We don't know your story. I don't know why you're sitting on a beach, drinking alone, and living in an RV in Horrorville, but you were a cop. You worked on a grisly case and you must have been good, or your Sergeant wouldn't have sent us."

"I know why he sent you," she said, before taking another swig.

"So why not help us?" asked Daniels. "Look over—"

"No," she said, standing and wobbling slightly. "I'm going to pick up my gun. Don't shoot me." She leaned over and picked up her weapon and tucked it back in her shorts. "Good luck with your case." Turning, she walked back toward the waves, never looking back, and assumed her former position with the waves crashing over her feet.

"Son-of-a..." said Rem, turning toward Daniels. "What the hell's the matter with her?"

"A lot," said Daniels. "I think a lot is the matter with her. She's done. Like we thought. Burned out."

"It's more than that," said Rem. "Did you see her when she pulled her weapon?"

"Quite vividly," said Daniels.

"Did you see her eyes?"

"I was more focused on preventing her from shooting you."

Rem paused. "I could see it. I think she's terrified."

Daniels watched Jill, standing in the surf and drinking her beer.

"Whatever happened, it wasn't good," said Rem.

"That's probably why she threatens to shoot strangers."

Rem put his badge back in his pocket. "I don't think she was expecting us. She was expecting someone else."

Daniels shook his head. Rem patted Daniels on the arm. "Let's go."

Lozano stared at his apple for the hundredth time that day. He'd had his roasted chicken, cauliflower potatoes and grilled veggies for lunch, but his stomach rumbled. This low-salt, low-sugar diet his doctor had recommended was going to kill him before this job ever would. But his high cholesterol and higher blood pressure were saying otherwise. He needed to lose about twenty pounds. So far, he'd lost seven. Rem had invited him to the gym to spar, and Daniels had offered to take him to lift weights, but he'd declined both offers. He saw his detectives enough as it was. He didn't need to work out with them. Lozano opened his drawer and saw the loose change. The vending machine beckoned down the hall.

A knock on his open door made him close the drawer. Remalla stood there grinning. "What you doin', Cap?" He pulled a candy bar out of his pocket and started to open it.

Lozano's stomach rumbled again. "Mind your business, Remalla."

Daniels walked up behind Remalla. "You got a sec, Cap?" He saw the chocolate in Rem's hands and rolled his eyes.

"I do. Have a seat. How'd it go with Jacobs?"

The detectives sat, and Daniels pointed at the apple. "You gonna eat that?"

Lozano eyed the fruit and his detective. He sighed, picked up the apple and tossed it. "It's all yours."

"Thanks," said Daniels, and he took a bite.

"Jacobs was a total bust," said Rem as he licked the chocolate off his thumb. "She has no interest in helping us."

"She's a recluse," said Daniels. "She lives in a run-down RV park, drinks a lot and waves guns at people. I'm not sure why Merchant recommended her."

Lozano sighed and sat back in his seat. "I know why. I talked to Merchant and got her file."

Rem paused before taking the next bite of his candy. "Really? Now I'm curious."

Lozano tapped on his keyboard and the monitor came to life. "I'm going to send you the info, but in a nutshell, she's the youngest female promoted to a detective on the Seattle force. She rose quickly in the ranks. Scored high in every area. She was book smart and street smart. Her father is a Federal judge. Did you know that?"

Daniels leaned forward. "That didn't come up in the conversation."

"The honorable Thomas Jack Jacobs. Known as—"

Daniels raised a brow. "Jailtime Jacobs?"

"The one and the same," said Lozano.

"I've heard of him," said Daniels.

Rem shot Daniels a puzzled look. "Since when are you familiar with the Seattle judicial branch?"

"You remember when I took that course on criminal law? They mentioned him. His harsh sentences are legendary. He's famous in Seattle law enforcement." He studied his apple. "Jill's his daughter?"

"She is," said Lozano. "Probably why she was so impressive on the force."

"Like father, like daughter," said Rem, as he took another bite of his candy bar.

"Anyway, when the killings started in Seattle, the city was in an uproar. Merchant had a slew of detectives on it. But he was dealing with the same issues as us. No prints, no DNA, nothing. The guy was a ghost."

"Wonderful," said Rem.

"Jacobs was a policewoman, but her ideas and observations about the killer caught Merchant's attention. Said she was like a profiler. She could almost predict the killer's next steps. By then, they had three victims and Merchant needed a plan, so he promoted her to detective and put her on the case. At that point, they were keeping the press at bay, but Jacob's had her own ideas. She wanted to use the press to draw him out. Merchant wasn't convinced. Not long after her promotion, Jacob's took it upon herself to hold a mini press conference outside one of the victim's homes. Called the killer..." he studied the screen, "...frightened, disturbed, with a slew of sexual issues." He sat back. "You get the gist."

Daniels chewed and swallowed another bite of his apple. "I don't know if that makes her brilliant or incredibly stupid."

"It certainly makes her fearless," said Rem. He popped the last bit of candy in his mouth. "How'd that go over with Merchant?"

"Not well," said Lozano. He laced his fingers together and put his hands behind his head. "It pissed off the higher-ups, and Merchant took the heat. But that's when the writing on the walls started."

Daniels' eyes widened. "Really?"

"Really," said Lozano. "After the next victim, the first message appeared, written on the bathroom wall in the victim's blood. It said, 'I see you.' There was also a rose."

"A rose?" asked Rem. He licked chocolate off the rest of his fingers. "What rose?"

"At the crime scene. The killer left a rose in the tub, and on the wall above it, written in blood, were the words 'For you.'"

"You got to be kidding me," said Daniels. "I didn't hear that."

"Seattle PD never released it to the press, for obvious reasons," said Lozano. "They kept it under wraps. Once we get the files from Seattle, you'll read all about it."

"And they think the killer was referring to Jacobs?" asked Rem. "Those messages were for her?"

"I guess her portrayal of him got his attention," said Daniels. "What exactly was she hoping to accomplish by pushing his buttons?"

"Probably exactly that," said Rem. "Get the guy to do something stupid. Something different from his routine and pray he makes a mistake."

"It worked," said Lozano. He opened his top drawer and pulled out a granola bar. His planned foray to the vending machine would have to wait. "Problem is, it worked too well."

Rem wiped his fingers on his jeans. "It got him to change his routine, but he didn't make a mistake. Only now, Jill's in his crosshairs."

"Right," said Lozano, as he opened the granola bar. "According to the file, not long after, Jill started receiving mail, flowers, phone calls, all from the killer."

Rem leaned forward and put his elbows on his knees. "Wow. He started contacting her?"

"And following her. He sent photos, too," said Lozano.

"Shit," said Daniels.

"And with all of that, they still couldn't catch this guy?" asked Rem. "It seems she gave Merchant exactly what he needed. Between the contact and photos, they couldn't nail him down? If nothing else, they could follow Jacobs."

"They did it all," said Lozano. "The phone calls were too short to trace, and if they weren't, the killer was long gone before they got there. No prints or DNA on the letters. Following Jill led nowhere. It was like he found a new way to taunt them, and he was having fun with it."

"And torturing Jacobs at the same time," said Daniels. He took a last bite of his apple and tossed it in the trash.

"Merchant said she handled it pretty well at first. She thought like most of them that it would lead to his capture. If she could just keep up the game, he would screw up. She played her part, talking to him, and trying to get him riled enough to slip up. Merchant put a detail on her to keep watch even though Jacobs argued with him about it. Said it would be hard to lure the murderer out if she was being followed all the time. Merchant argued back that he didn't need a dead cop on his hands."

Daniels let out a sigh. "Brave lady."

"I'm sensing this didn't end well," said Rem.

"You should be a detective," said Daniels.

Rem smirked.

"You're right, it didn't," said Lozano. He held his granola bar. "The murders continued, as did the messages. More notes to Jill at the crime scene. More photos and phone calls. Crazy thing is, Jill had an uncanny sense about the guy. Merchant said she knew when he would strike again and could almost sense the killer's and victim's pain. She lost weight, spent sleepless nights working, and yelled at other cops when they didn't keep the same regimen. The respect she'd garnered through all of this began to wane. Merchant said after a while, the stress on the department began to cause fractures. There were grumblings that maybe Jill knew the killer all along. Maybe she was in on it, which is why she could predict his actions. Maybe she liked the attention, so she strung everyone along, not telling them everything she knew."

Rem rubbed his face and stood. A strand of hair fell in his face and he pushed it back. "That's great. She's killing herself to find this guy and her department's turning on her." He leaned against the wall and crossed his arms.

"What did Merchant do?" asked Daniels.

"He defended her. Did his best to protect her. Most knew none of the rumors were true, but the squad was just tired and fed up. They wanted a scapegoat."

"They couldn't get the killer, so they had to blame somebody," said Daniels.

"It seems so. But according to Merchant, the more he told Jacobs to slow down and take a break, the harder she worked. She ignored the rumors, but at some point, the cracks showed. Arguments broke out on the job. She became less and less tolerant of her fellow officers and more belligerent with him. She even lost it with the killer. He'd called her, and she'd let loose, daring him to come for her, saying he didn't have the balls to kill her. Merchant took her off the case after that."

Rem cursed under his breath. "This story just keeps getting better and better. How'd she handle being taken off the case?"

"About as well as you can imagine," said Lozano.

"Merchant was right. She was in too deep," said Daniels.

"Is that when she left?" asked Rem.

"No," said Lozano. He paused and stared at his granola bar. He'd yet to take a bite. "Three days later, a policeman was killed." He studied his monitor. "Officer Rick Henderson. They found him in a bathtub, stabbed, his face painted. There were notes written on the walls to Jacobs, telling her it was all for her."

Rem stared at the floor, and Daniels leaned back, rubbing his eyes. "Holy shit," he said.

"That's when Jacobs left the force, and hasn't been back," said Lozano. "That was the last murder. The killer went silent afterwards. It was as if he'd had his fun with her and when she left, he did too. Until six weeks ago."

Neither detective spoke.

"So, if you're wondering why she's not too social, drinks a lot, and pulls guns on people," said Lozano, "now you know."

Daniels nodded and sighed. "And now the killer's back and he's picked our little corner of the world to prey upon," said Daniels. "Lucky us."

Rem raised his head. "But now we know why."

Daniels shared a look with Rem, and his brow furrowed. "He's come back for her.